Wallflower:
Fidelity in Adversity

A murder had occurred
at her aunt's inn, and
Autumn Gallegher had
evidence—on film. Though the
victim had been an evil person,
something had to be done.
Could she develop the pictures
when she believed she knew
who the murderer was?
Faithful in adversity, Autumn
could not betray the man she
loved.

NORA ROBERTS

LANGUAGE OF LOVE

**Love has a language all its own, and for
centuries, flowers have symbolized
love's finest expression.
Discover the language of flowers
—and love—
in this romantic collection of 48 favorite
books by bestselling author Nora Roberts.**

NORA ROBERTS

LANGUAGE OF LOVE

STORM WARNING

Silhouette Books ®

For Mom,
Who wouldn't let my brothers clobber me—even
when I deserved it

SILHOUETTE BOOKS
300 East 42nd St., New York, N.Y. 10017

STORM WARNING © 1984 by Nora Roberts.
First published as a Silhouette Romance.

Language of Love edition published March 1992.

ISBN: 0-373-51004-7

Printed in U.S.A.

Chapter One

The Pine View Inn was nestled comfortably in the Blue Ridge Mountains. After leaving the main road, the meandering driveway crossed a narrow ford just wide enough for one car. The inn was situated a short distance beyond the ford.

It was a lovely place, full of character, the lines so clean they disguised the building's rambling structure. It was three stories high, built of brick that had been weathered to a soft rose, the facade interspersed with narrow, white-shuttered windows. The hipped roof had faded long ago to a quiet green, and three straight chimneys rose from it. A wide wooden porch made a white skirt around the entire house and doors opened out to it from all four sides.

The surrounding lawn was smooth and well tended. There was less than an acre, house included, before the trees and outcroppings of rock staked their claim on the land. It was as if nature had decided that the house could have this much and no more. The effect was magnificent. The house and mountains stood in peaceful coexistence, neither detracting from the other's beauty.

As she pulled her car to the informal parking area at the side of the house, Autumn counted five cars, including her aunt's vintage Chevy. Though the season was still weeks off, it appeared that the inn already had several guests.

There was a light April chill in the air. The daffodils had yet to open, and the crocuses were just beginning to fade. A few azalea buds showed a trace of color. The day was poised and waiting for spring. The higher, surrounding mountains clung to their winter brown, but touches of green were creeping up them. It wouldn't be gloomy brown and gray for long.

Autumn swung her camera case over one shoulder and her purse over the other—the purse was of secondary importance. Two large suitcases also had to be dragged from the trunk. After a moment's struggle, she managed to arrange everything so that she could take it all in one load, then mounted the steps. The door, as always, was unlocked.

There was no one about. The sprawling living room which served as a lounge was empty, though a fire crackled in the grate. Setting down her cases, Autumn entered the room. Nothing had changed.

Rag rugs dotted the floor; hand-crocheted afghans were draped on the two patchworked sofas. At the windows were chintz priscillas and the Hummel collection was still on the mantel. Characteristically, the room was neat, but far from orderly. There were magazines here and there, an overflowing sewing basket, a group of pillows piled for comfort rather than style on the windowseat. The ambience was friendly with a faintly distracted charm. Autumn thought with a smile that the room suited her aunt perfectly.

She felt an odd pleasure. It was always reassuring to find that something loved hasn't changed. Taking a last quick glance around the room, she ran a hand through her hair. It hung past her waist and was tousled from the long drive with open windows. She gave idle consideration to digging out a brush, but promptly forgot when she heard footsteps down the hall.

"Oh, Autumn, there you are." Typically, her aunt greeted her as though Autumn had just spent an hour at the local supermarket rather than a year in New York. "I'm glad you got in before dinner. We're having pot roast, your favorite."

Not having the heart to remind her aunt that pot roast was her brother Paul's favorite, Autumn smiled. "Aunt Tabby, it's so good to see you!" Quickly she walked over and kissed her aunt's cheek. The familiar scent of lavender surrounded her.

Aunt Tabby in no way resembled the cat her name brought to mind. Cats are prone to snobbishness, disdainfully tolerating the rest of the world. They are known for speed, agility and cunning. Aunt Tabby was known for her vague meanderings, disjointed conversations and confused thinking. She had no guile. Autumn adored her.

Drawing her aunt away, Autumn studied her closely. "You look wonderful." It was invariably true. Aunt Tabby's hair was the same deep chestnut as her niece's, but it was liberally dashed with gray. It suited her. She wore it short, curling haphazardly around her small round face. Her features were all small-scaled—mouth, nose, ears, even her hands and feet. Her eyes were a mistily faded blue. Though she was halfway through her fifties, her skin refused to wrinkle; it was smooth as a girl's. She stood a half-foot shorter than Autumn and was pleasantly round and soft. Beside her, Autumn felt like a gangly toothpick.

Autumn hugged her again, then kissed her other cheek. "Absolutely wonderful."

Aunt Tabby smiled up at her. "What a pretty girl you are. I always knew you would be. But so awfully thin." She patted Autumn's cheek and wondered how many calories were in pot roast.

With a shrug, Autumn thought of the ten pounds she had gained when she'd stopped smoking. She had lost them again almost as quickly.

"Nelson always was thin," Aunt Tabby added, thinking of her brother, Autumn's father.

"Still is," Autumn told her. She set her camera case on a table and grinned at her aunt. "Mom's always threatening to sue for divorce."

"Oh well." Aunt Tabby clucked her tongue and looked thoughtful. "I don't think that's wise after all the years they've been married." Knowing the jest had been lost, Autumn merely nodded in agreement. "I gave you the room you always liked, dear. You can still see the lake from the window. The leaves will be full soon though, but... Remember when you fell in when you were a little girl? Nelson had to fish you out."

"That was Will," Autumn reminded her, thinking back on the day her younger brother had toppled into the lake.

"Oh?" Aunt Tabby looked faintly confused a moment, then smiled disarmingly. "He learned to swim quite well, didn't he? Such an enormous young man now. It always surprised me. There aren't any children with us at the moment," she added, flowing from sentence to sentence with her own brand of logic.

"I saw several cars. Are there many people here?" Autumn stretched her cramped muscles as she wandered the room. It smelled of sandalwood and lemon oil.

"One double and five singles," she told her. "One of the singles is French and quite fond of my apple pie. I must go check on my blueberry cobbler," she announced suddenly. "Nancy is a marvel with a pot roast, but helpless with baking. George is down with a virus."

She was already making for the door as Autumn tried to puzzle out the last snatch of information.

"I'm sorry to hear that," she replied with what she hoped was appropriate sympathy.

"I'm a bit shorthanded at the moment, dear, so perhaps you can manage your suitcases yourself. Or you can wait for one of the gentlemen to come in."

George, Autumn remembered. Gardener, bellboy and bartender.

"Don't worry, Aunt Tabby. I can manage."

"Oh, by the way, Autumn." She turned back, but Autumn knew her aunt's thoughts were centered on the fate of her cobbler. "I have a little surprise for you—oh, I see Miss Bond is coming in." Typically, she interrupted herself, then smiled. "She'll keep you company. Dinner's at the usual time. Don't be late."

Obviously relieved that both her cobbler and her niece were about to be taken care of, she bustled off, her heels tapping cheerfully on the hardwood floor.

Autumn turned to watch her designated companion enter through the side door. She found herself gaping.

Julia Bond. Of course, Autumn recognized her instantly. There could be no other woman who possessed such shimmering, golden beauty. How many times had she sat in a crowded theater and watched Julia's charm and talent transcend the movie screen? In person, in the flesh, her beauty didn't diminish. It sparkled, all the more alive in three dimensions.

Small, with exquisite curves just bordering on lush, Julia Bond was a magnificent example of womanhood at its best. Her cream-colored linen slacks and vivid blue cashmere sweater set off her coloring to perfection. Pale golden hair framed her face like sunlight. Her eyes were a deep summer blue. The full, shapely mouth lifted into a smile even as the famous brows arched. For a moment, Julia stood, fingering her silk scarf. Then she spoke, her voice smoky, exactly as Autumn had known it would be. "What fabulous hair."

It took Autumn a moment to register the comment. Her mind was blank at seeing Julia Bond step into her aunt's lounge as casually as she would have strolled into the New York Hilton. The smile, however, was full of charm and so completely unaffected that Autumn was able to form one in return.

"Thank you. I'm sure you're used to being stared at, Miss Bond, but I apologize anyway."

Julia sat, with a grace that was at once insolent and admirable, in a wingback chair. Drawing out a long, thin cigarette, she gave Autumn a full-power smile. "Actors adore being stared at. Sit down." She gestured. "I have a feeling I've at last found someone to talk to in this place."

Autumn's obedience was automatic, a tribute to the actress's charm.

"Of course," Julia continued, still studying Autumn's face, "you're entirely too young and too attractive." Settling back, she crossed her legs. Somehow, she managed to transform the wingback chair, with the small darning marks in the left arm, into a throne. "Then your coloring and mine offset each other nicely. How old are you, darling?"

"Twenty-five." Captivated, Autumn answered without thinking.

Julia laughed, a low bubbling sound that flowed and ebbed like a wave. "Oh, so am I. Perennially." She tossed her head in amusement, then left it cocked to the side. Autumn's fingers itched for her camera. "What's your name, darling, and what brings you to solitude and pine trees?"

"Autumn," she responded as she pushed her hair off her shoulders. "Autumn Gallegher. My aunt owns the inn."

"Your aunt?" Julia's face registered surprise and more amusement. "That dear fuzzy little lady is your aunt?"

"Yes." A grin escaped at the accuracy of the description. "My father's sister." Relaxed, Autumn leaned back. She was doing her own studying, thinking in angles and shadings.

"Incredible," Julia decided with a shake of her head. "You don't look like her. Oh, the hair," she corrected with an envious glance. "I imagine hers was once your color. Magnificent. I know women who would kill for that shade, and you seem to have about three feet of it." With a sigh, she drew delicately on her cigarette. "So, you've come to pay your aunt a visit."

There was nothing condescending in her attitude. Her eyes were interested and Autumn began to find her not only charming but likable. "For a few weeks. I haven't seen her in nearly a year. She wrote and asked me to come down, so I'm taking my vacation all at one time."

"What do you do?" Julia pursed her lips. "Model?"

"No." Autumn's laughter came quickly at the thought of it. "I'm a photographer."

"Photographer!" Julia exclaimed. She glowed with pleasure. "I'm very fond of photographers. Vanity, I suppose."

"I imagine photographers are fond of you for the same reason."

"Oh, my dear." When Julia smiled, Autumn recognized both pleasure and amusement. "How sweet."

"Are you alone, Miss Bond?" Her sense of curiosity was ingrained. Autumn had already forgotten to be overwhelmed.

"Julia, please, or you'll remind me of the half-decade that separates our ages. The color of that sweater suits you," she commented, eyeing Autumn's crewneck. "I never could wear gray. Sorry, darling," she apologized with a lightning-quick smile. "Clothes are a weakness of mine. Am I alone?" The smile deepened. "Actually, this little hiatus is a mixture of business and pleasure. I'm in between husbands at the moment—a glorious interlude." Julia tossed her head. "Men are delightful, but husbands can be dreadfully inhibiting. Have you ever had one?"

"No." The grin was irrepressible. From the tone, Julia might have asked if Autumn had ever owned a cocker spaniel.

"I've had three." Julia's eyes grew wicked and delighted. "In this case, the third was *not* the charm. Six months with an English baron was quite enough."

Autumn remembered the photos she had seen of Julia with a tall, aristocratic Englishman. She had worn tweed brilliantly.

"I've taken a vow of abstinence," Julia continued. "Not against men—against marriage."

"Until the next time?" Autumn ventured.

"Until the next time," Julia agreed with a laugh. "At the moment, I'm here for platonic purposes with Jacques LeFarre."

"The producer?"

"Of course." Again, Autumn felt the close scrutiny. "He'll take one look at you and decide he has a new star on the horizon. Still, that might be an interesting diversion." She frowned a moment, then shrugged it away. "The other residents of your aunt's cozy inn have offered little in the way of diversions thus far."

"Oh?" Automatically, Autumn shook her head as Julia offered her a cigarette.

"We have Dr. and Mrs. Spicer," Julia began. One perfectly shaped nail tapped against the arm of her chair. There was something different in her attitude now. Autumn was sensitive to moods, but this was too subtle a change for her to identify. "The doctor himself might be interesting," Julia continued. "He's very tall and nicely built, smoothly handsome with just the right amount of gray at the temples."

She smiled. Just then Autumn thought Julia resembled a very pretty, well-fed cat.

"The wife is short and unfortunately rather dumpy. She spoils whatever attractiveness she might have with a continually morose expression." Julia demonstrated it with terrifying skill. Autumn's laughter burst out before she could stop it.

"How unkind," Autumn chided, smiling still.

"Oh, I know." A graceful hand waved in dismissal. "I have no patience for women who let themselves go, then look daggers at those who don't. He's fond of fresh air and walking in the woods, and she grumbles and mopes along after him." Julia paused, giving Autumn a wary glance. "How do you feel about walking?"

"I like it." Hearing the apology in her voice, Autumn grinned.

"Oh well." Julia shrugged at eccentricities. "It takes all kinds. Next, we have Helen Easterman." The oval, tinted nails began to tap again. Her eyes drifted from Autumn's to the view out the window. Somehow, Autumn didn't think she was seeing mountains and pine trees. "She says she's an art teacher, taking time off to sketch nature. She's rather attractive, though a bit overripe, with sharp little eyes and an unpleasant smile. Then, there's Steve Anderson." Julia gave her slow, cat smile again. Describing men, Autumn mused, was more to her taste. "He's rather delicious. Wide shoulders, California blond hair. Nice blue eyes. And he's embarrassingly rich. His father owns, ah . . ."

"Anderson Manufacturing?" Autumn prompted and was rewarded with a beam of approval.

"How clever of you."

"I heard something about Steve Anderson aiming for a political career."

"Mmm, yes. It would suit him." Julia nodded. "He's very well-mannered and has a disarmingly boyish smile—that's always a political asset."

"It's a sobering thought that government officials are elected on their smiles."

"Oh, politics." Julia wrinkled her nose and shrugged away the entire profession. "I had an affair with a senator once. Nasty business, politics." She laughed at some private joke.

Not certain whether her comment had been a romantic observation or a general one, Autumn didn't pursue it. "So far," Autumn said, "it seems an unlikely menagerie for Julia Bond and Jacques LeFarre to join."

"Show business." With a smile, she lit another cigarette, then waved it at Autumn. "Stick with photography, Autumn, no matter what promises Jacques makes you. We're here due to a whim of the last and most interesting character in our little play. He's a genius of a writer. I did one of his screenplays a few years back. Jacques wants to produce another, and he wants me for the lead." She dragged deep on the cigarette. "I'm willing—really good scripts aren't that easy to come by—but our writer is in the middle of a novel. Jacques thinks the novel could be turned into a screenplay, but our genius resists. He told Jacques he was coming here to write in peace for a few weeks, and that he'd think it over. The charming LeFarre talked him into allowing us to join him for a few days."

Autumn was both fascinated and confused. Her question was characteristically blunt. "Do you usually chase writers around this way? I'd think it would be more the other way around."

"And you'd be right," Julia said flatly. With only the movement of her eyebrows, her expression turned haughty. "But Jacques is dead set on producing this man's work, and he caught me at a weak moment. I had just finished reading one of the most appalling scripts. Actually," she amended with a grimace, "three of the most appalling scripts. My work feeds me, but I won't do trash. So..." Julia smiled and moved her hands. "Here I am."

"Chasing a reluctant writer."

"It has its compensations."

I'd like to shoot her with the sun at her back. Low sun, just going down. The contrasts would be perfect. Autumn pulled herself back from her thoughts and caught up with Julia's conversation. "Compensations?" she repeated.

"The writer happens to be incredibly attractive, in that carelessly rugged sort of way that no one can pull off unless he's born with it. A marvelous change of pace," she added with a wicked gleam, "from English barons. He's tall and bronzed with black hair that's just a bit too long and always disheveled. It makes a woman itch to get her fingers into it. Best, he has those dark eyes that say 'go to hell' so eloquently. He's an arrogant devil." Her sigh was pure feminine approval. "Arrogant men are irresistible, don't you think?"

Autumn murmured something while she tried to block out the suspicions Julia's words were forming. It had to be someone else, she thought frantically. Anyone else.

"And, of course, Lucas McLean's talent deserves a bit of arrogance."

The color drained from Autumn's face and left it stiff. Waves of almost forgotten pain washed over her. *How could it hurt so much after all this time?* She had built the wall so carefully, so laboriously—how could it crumble into dust at the sound of a name? She wondered, dully, what sadistic quirk of fate had brought Lucas McLean back to torment her.

"Why, darling, what's the matter?"

Julia's voice, mixed with concern and curiosity, penetrated. As if coming up for air, Autumn shook her head. "Nothing." She shook her head again and swallowed. "It was just a surprise to hear that Lucas McLean is here." Drawing a deep breath, she met Julia's eyes. "I knew him . . . a long time ago."

"Oh, I see."

And she did see, Autumn noted, very well. Sympathy warred with speculation in both her face and voice. Autumn shrugged, determined to treat it lightly.

"I doubt he remembers me." Part of her prayed with fervor it was true, while another prayed at cross-purposes. Would he forget? she wondered. Could he?

"Autumn, darling, yours is a face no man is likely to forget." Through a mist of smoke, Julia studied her. "You were very young when you fell in love with him?"

"Yes." Autumn was trying, painfully, to rebuild her protective wall and wasn't surprised by the question. "Too young, too naive." She managed a brittle smile and for the first time in six months accepted a cigarette. "But I learn quickly."

"It seems the next few days might prove interesting, after all."

"Yes." Autumn's agreement lacked enthusiasm. "So it does." She needed time to be alone, to steady herself. "I have to take my bags up," she said as she rose.

While Autumn stretched her slender arms toward the ceiling, Julia smiled. "I'll see you at dinner."

Nodding, Autumn gathered up her camera case and purse and left the room.

In the hall, she struggled with her suitcases, camera and purse before beginning the task of transporting them up the stairs. Throughout the slow trek up the stairs, Autumn relieved tension by muttering and swearing. *Lucas McLean,* she thought and banged a suitcase against her shin. She nearly convinced herself that her ill humor was a result of the bruise she'd just given herself. Out of breath and patience, she reached the hallway outside her room and dumped everything on the floor with an angry thud.

"Hello, Cat. No bellboy?"

The voice—and the ridiculous nickname—knocked a few of her freshly mortared bricks loose. After a brief hesitation, Autumn turned to him. The pain wouldn't show on her face. She'd learned that much. But the pain was there, surprisingly real and physical. It reminded her of the day her brother had swung a baseball bat into her stomach when she had been twelve. *I'm not twelve now,* she reminded herself. She met Lucas's arrogant smile with one of her own.

"Hello, Lucas. I heard you were here. The Pine View Inn is bursting with celebrities."

He was the same, she noted. Dark and lean and male. There was a ruggedness about him, accented by rough black brows and craggy, demanding features that couldn't be called handsome. Oh, no, that was much too tame a word for Lucas McLean. Arousing, irresistible. Fatal. Those words suited him better.

His eyes were nearly as black as his hair. They kept secrets easily. He carried himself well, with a negligent grace that was natural rather than studied. His not-so-subtle masculine power drifted with him as he ambled closer and studied her.

It was then that Autumn noticed how hellishly tired he looked. There were shadows under his eyes. He needed a shave. The creases in his cheeks were deeper than she remembered— and she remembered very well.

"You look like yesterday." He grabbed a handful of her hair as he fastened his eyes on hers. She wondered how she could have ever thought herself over him. No woman ever got over Lucas. Sheer determination kept her eyes level.

"You," she countered as she opened her door, "look like hell. You need some sleep."

Lucas leaned on the doorjamb before she could drag her cases inside and slam the door. "Having trouble with one of my characters," he said smoothly. "She's a tall, willowy creature with chestnut hair that ripples down her back. Narrow hipped, with legs that go right up to her waist."

Bracing herself, Autumn turned back and stared at him. Carefully, she erased any expression from her face.

"She has a child's mouth," he continued, dropping his glance to hers a moment. "And a small nose, somewhat at odds with high, elegant cheekbones. Her skin is ivory with touches of warmth just under the surface. Her eyes are long lidded and ridiculously lashed—green that melts into amber, like a cat's."

Without comment, she listened to his description of herself. She gave him a bored, disinterested look he would never have seen on her face three years before. "Is she the murderer or the corpse?" It pleased Autumn to see his brows lift in surprise before they drew together in a frown.

"I'll send you a copy when it's done." He searched her face, then a shutter came down, leaving his expression unreadable. That, too, she noted, hadn't changed.

"You do that." After giving her cases a superhuman tug, jettisoning them into her room, Autumn rested against the door. Her smile had no feeling. "You'll have to excuse me, Lucas, I've had a long drive and want a bath."

She closed the door firmly and with finality, in his face.

Autumn's movements then became brisk. There was unpacking to do and a bath to draw and a dress to choose for dinner. Those things would give her time to recover before she allowed herself to think, to feel. When she slipped into lingerie and stockings, her nerves were steadier. The worst of it had been weathered. Surely, she mused, the first meeting, the first exchange of words were the most difficult. She had seen him. She had spoken to him. She had survived. Success made her bold. For the first time in nearly two years, Autumn allowed herself to remember.

She had been so much in love. Her assignment had been an ordinary one—a picture layout of mystery novelist Lucas McLean. The result had been six months of incredible joy followed by unspeakable hurt.

He had overwhelmed her. She'd never met anyone like him. She knew now that there was no one else like him. He was a law unto himself. He had been brilliant, compelling, selfish and moody. After the first shock of learning he was interested in her, Autumn had floated along on a cloud of wonder and admiration. And love.

His arrogance, as Julia had said, was irresistible. His phone calls at three in the morning had been treasured. The last time she had been held in his arms, experiencing the wild demands of his mouth, had been as exciting as the first. She had tumbled into his bed like a ripe peach, giving up her innocence with the freedom that comes with blind, trusting love.

She remembered he'd never said the words she wanted to hear. She'd told herself she had no need for them—words weren't important. There were unexpected boxes of roses, surprise picnics on the beach with wine in paper cups and lovemaking that was both intense and all consuming. What did she need with words? When the end had come it had been swift—but far from painless.

Autumn put his distraction, his moodiness down to trouble with the novel he was working on. It didn't occur to her that he'd been bored. It was her habit to fix dinner on Wednesdays at his home. It was a small, private evening, one she prized above all others. Her arrival was so natural to her, so routine, that when she entered his living room and found him dressed in dinner clothes, she only thought he had decided to add a more formal atmosphere to their quiet dinner.

"Why, Cat, what are you doing here?" The unexpected words were spoken so easily, she merely stared. "Ah, it's Wednesday, isn't it?" There was a slight annoyance in his tone, as though he had forgotten a dentist appointment. "I completely forgot. I'm afraid I've made other plans."

"Other plans?" she echoed. Comprehension was still a long way off.

"I should have phoned you and saved you the trip. Sorry, Cat, I'm just leaving."

"Leaving?"

"I'm going out." He moved across the room and stared at her. She shivered. No one's eyes could be as warm—or as cold—as Lucas McLean's. "Don't be difficult, Autumn, I don't want to hurt you any more than is necessary."

Feeling the tears of realization rush out, she shook her head and fought against acceptance. The tears sent him into a fury.

"Stop it! I haven't the time to deal with weeping. Just pack it in. Chalk it up to experience. God knows you need it."

Swearing, he stomped away to light a cigarette. She had stood there, weeping without sound.

"Don't make a fool of yourself, Autumn." The calm, rigid voice was more frightening to her than his anger. At least anger was an emotion. "When something's over, you forget it and move on." He turned back with a shrug. "That's life."

"You don't want me anymore?" She stood meekly, like a dog who waits to feel the lash again. Her vision was too clouded with tears to see his expression. For a moment, he was silent.

"Don't worry, Cat," he answered in a careless, brutal voice. "Others will."

She turned and fled. It had taken over a year before he had stopped being the first thing in her mind every morning.

But she had survived, she reminded herself. She slipped into a vivid green dress. *And I'll keep right on surviving.* She knew she was basically the same person who had fallen in love with Lucas, but now she had a more polished veneer. Innocence was gone, and it would take more than Lucas McLean to make a fool of her again. She tossed her head, satisfied with the memory of her reception to him. That had given him a bit of a surprise. No, Autumn Gallegher was no one's fool any longer.

Her thoughts drifted to her aunt's odd assortment of guests. She wondered briefly why the rich and famous were gathering here instead of at some exclusive resort. Dismissing the thought with a shrug, she reminded herself it was dinnertime. Aunt Tabby had told her not to be late.

Chapter Two

It was a strange assortment to find clustered in the lounge of a remote Virginia inn: an award-winning writer, an actress, a producer, a wealthy California businessman, a successful cardiovascular surgeon and his wife, an art teacher who wore St. Laurent. Before Autumn's bearings were complete, she found herself enveloped in them. Julia pounced on her possessively and began introductions. Obviously, Julia enjoyed her prior claim and the center-stage position it gave her. Whatever embarrassment Autumn might have felt at being thrust into the limelight was overridden by amusement at the accuracy of Julia's earlier descriptions.

Dr. Robert Spicer was indeed smoothly handsome. He was drifting toward fifty and bursting with health. He wore a casually expensive green cardigan with brown leather patches at the elbows. His wife, Jane, was also as Julia had described: unfortunately dumpy. The small smile she gave Autumn lasted about two seconds before her face slipped back into the dissatisfied grooves that were habitual. She cast dark, bad-tempered glances at her husband while he gave Julia the bulk of his attention.

Watching them, Autumn could find little sympathy for Jane and no disapproval for Julia—no one disapproves of a flower for drawing bees. Julia's attraction was just as natural, and just as potent.

Helen Easterman was attractive in a slick, practiced fashion. The scarlet of her dress suited her, but struck a jarring note in the simply furnished lounge. Her face was perfectly made-up and reminded Autumn of a mask. As a photographer, she knew the tricks and secrets of cosmetics. Instinctively, Autumn avoided her.

In contrast, Steve Anderson was all charm. Good looks, California style, as Julia had said. Autumn liked the crinkles at the corners of his eyes and his careless chic. He wore chinos easily. From his bearing, she knew he would wear black tie with equal aplomb. If he chose a political career, she mused, he should make his way very well.

Julia had offered no description of Jacques LeFarre. What Autumn knew of him came primarily from either the gossip magazines or his films. He was smaller than she had imagined, barely as tall as she, but with a wiry build. His features were strong and he wore his brown hair brushed back from his forehead where three worry lines had been etched. She liked the trim moustache over his mouth, and the way he lifted her hand to kiss it when they were introduced.

"Well, Autumn," Steve began with a smile. "I'm playing bartender in George's absence. What can I fix you?"

"Vodka Collins, easy on the vodka," Lucas answered. Autumn gave up the idea of ignoring him.

"Your memory's improved," she said coolly.

"So's your wardrobe." He ran a finger down the collar of her dress. "I remember when it ran to jeans and old sweaters."

"I grew up." Her eyes were as steady and as measuring as his.

"So I see."

"Ah, you have met before," Jacques put in. "But this is fascinating. You are old friends?"

"Old friends?" Lucas repeated before Autumn could speak. He studied her with infuriating amusement. "Would you say that was an accurate description, Cat?"

"Cat?" Jacques frowned a moment. "Ah, the eyes, *oui.*" Pleased, he brushed his index finger over his moustache. "It suits. What do you think, *chérie?*" He turned to Julia, who seemed to be enjoying herself watching the unfolding scene. "She's enchanting, and her voice is quite good."

"I've already warned Autumn about you," Julia drawled, then gave Robert Spicer a glorious smile.

"Ah, Julia," Jacques said mildly, "how wicked of you."

"Autumn works the other side of the camera," Lucas stated. Knowing his eyes had been on her the entire time, Autumn was grateful when Steve returned with her drink. "She's a photographer."

"Again, I'm fascinated." Autumn's free hand was captured in Jacques's. "Tell me why you are behind the camera instead of in front of it? Your hair alone would cause poets to run for their pens."

No woman was immune to flattery with a French accent, and Autumn smiled fully into his eyes. "I doubt I could stand still long enough to begin with."

"Photographers can be quite useful," Helen Easterman stated suddenly. Lifting a hand, she patted her dark, sleek cap of hair. "A good, clear photograph is an invaluable tool ... to an artist.''

An awkward pause followed the statement. Tension entered the room, so out of place in the comfortable lounge with its chintz curtains that Autumn thought it must be her imagination. Helen smiled into the silence and sipped her drink. Her eyes swept over the others, inclusively, never centering on one.

Autumn knew there was something here which isolated Helen and set her apart from the rest. Messages were being passed without words, though there was no way for Autumn to tell who was communicating what to whom. The mood changed swiftly as Julia engaged Robert Spicer in bright conversation. Jane Spicer's habitual frown became more pronounced.

The easy climate continued as they went in to dinner. Sitting between Jacques and Steve, Autumn was able to add to her education as she observed Julia flirting simultaneously with Lucas and Robert. She was, in Autumn's opinion, magnificent. Even through the discomfort of seeing Lucas casually return the flirtation, she had to admire Julia's talent. Her charm and beauty were insatiable. Jane ate in sullen silence.

Dreary woman, Autumn mused, then wondered what her own reaction would be if it were her husband so enchanted. Action, she decided, not silence. I'd simply claw her eyes out. The image of dumpy Jane wrestling with the elegant Julia made her smile. Even as she enjoyed the notion, she looked up to find Lucas's eyes on her.

His brows were lifted at an angle she knew meant amusement. Autumn turned her attention to Jacques.

"Do you find many differences in the movie industry here in America, Mr. LeFarre?"

"You must call me Jacques." His smile caused the tips of his moustache to rise. "There are differences, yes. I would say that Americans are more... adventurous than Europeans."

Autumn lifted her shoulders and smiled. "Maybe because we're a mixture of nationalities. Not watered down. Just Americanized."

"Americanized." Jacques tried out the word and approved it. His grin was younger than his smile, less urbane. "Yes, I would say I feel Americanized in California."

"Still, California's only one aspect of the country," Steve put in. "And I wouldn't call L.A. or southern California particularly typical." Autumn watched his eyes flick over her hair. His interest brought on a small flutter of response that pleased her. It proved that she was still a woman, open to a man—not just one man. "Have you ever been to California, Autumn?"

"I lived there...once." Her response to Steve, and the need to prove something to herself, urged her to turn her eyes to Lucas. Their gazes locked and held for one brief instant. "I relocated in New York three years ago."

"There was a family here from New York," Steve went on. If he'd noticed the look that had passed, he gave no sign. Yes, a good politician, Autumn thought again. "They just checked out this morning. The woman was one of those robust types with energy pouring out of every cell. She needed it," he added with a smile that was for Autumn alone. "She had three boys. Triplets. I think she said they were eleven."

"Oh, those beastly children!" Julia switched her attention from Robert and looked across the table. She rolled her summer blue eyes. "Running around like a pack of monkeys. Worse, you could never tell which one of them it was zooming by or leaping down. They did everything in triplicate." She shuddered and lifted her water glass. "They ate like elephants."

"Running and eating are part of child-hood," Jacques commented with a shake of his head. "Julia," he told Autumn with a con-spirator's wink, "was born twenty-one and beautiful."

"Anyone with manners is born twenty-one," Julia countered. "Being beautiful was simply a bonus." Her eyes were laughing now. "Jacques is crazy about kids," she informed Autumn. "He has three specimens of his own."

Interested, Autumn turned to him. She'd never thought of Jacques LeFarre in terms other than his work. "I'm crazy about them, too," she confessed and shot Julia a grin. "What sort of specimens do you have?"

"Boys," he answered. Autumn found the fondness in his eyes curiously touching. "They are like a ladder." With his hand, he formed imaginary steps. "Seven, eight and nine years. They live in France with my wife—my ex-wife." He frowned, then smoothed it away. Autumn realized how the worry lines in his brow had been formed.

"Jacques actually wants custody of the little monsters." Julia's look was more tolerant than her words. Here, Autumn saw, affection tran-scended flirtation. "Even though I hold your sanity suspect, Jacques, I'm forced to admit you make a better father than Claudette makes a mother."

"Custody suits are sensitive matters," Helen announced from the end of the table. She drank from her water glass, peering over the rim with small, sharp eyes. The look that she sent Jacques seemed to brush everyone else out of her line of vision. "It's so important that any . . . unsuitable information doesn't come to light."

Tension sprang back. Autumn felt the Frenchman stiffen beside her. But there was more. Undercurrents flowed up and down the long pine table. It was impossible not to feel them, though there was nothing tangible, nothing solid. Instinctively, Autumn's eyes sought Lucas's. There was nothing there but the hard, unfathomable mask she had seen too often in the past.

"Your aunt serves such marvelous meals, Miss Gallegher." With a puzzling, satisfied smirk, Helen shifted her attention to Autumn.

"Yes." She blundered into the awful silence. "Aunt Tabby gives food a high rating of importance."

"Aunt Tabby?" Julia's rich laugh warred with the tension, and won. The air was instantly lighter. "What a wonderful name. Did you know Autumn has an Aunt Tabby when you christened her Cat, Lucas?'' She stared up at him, her eyes wide and guileless. Autumn was reminded of a movie Julia had been in, in which she played the innocent ingenue to perfection.

"Lucas and I didn't know each other well enough to discuss relatives.'' Autumn's voice was easy and careless and pleased her very much. So did Lucas's barely perceptible frown.

"Actually,'' he replied, recovering quickly, "we were too occupied to discuss family trees.'' He sent her a smile which sneaked through her defenses. Autumn's pulse hammered. "What did we talk about in those days, Cat?''

"I've forgotten,'' she murmured, knowing she had lost the edge before she'd really held it. "It was a long time ago.''

Aunt Tabby bustled in with her prize cobbler.

There was music on the stereo and a muted fire in the hearth when they returned to the lounge. The scene, if Autumn could have captured it on film, was one of relaxed camaraderie. Steve and Robert huddled over a chessboard while Jane made her discontented way through a magazine. Even without a photographer's eye for color, Autumn knew the woman should never wear brown. She felt quite certain that Jane invariably would.

Lucas sprawled on the sofa. Somehow, he always managed to relax in a negligent fashion without seeming sloppy; there was always an alertness about him, energy simmering right under the surface. Autumn knew he watched people without being obvious—not because he cared if he made them uncomfortable, he didn't in the least—it was simply something he was able to do. And in watching them, he was able to learn their secrets. An obsessive writer, he drew his characters from flesh and blood. With no mercy, Autumn recalled.

At the moment, he seemed content with his conversation with Julia and Jacques. They flanked him on the sofa and spoke with the ease that came from familiarity; they shared the same world.

But it's not my world, Autumn reminded herself. I only pretended it was for a little while. I only pretended he was mine for a little while. She had been right when she told Lucas she had grown up. Pretend games were for children.

Yet, Autumn thought as she sat back and observed, there was a game of some sort going on here. There was a faint glistening of unease superimposed over the homey picture. Always attuned to contrasts, she could sense it, feel it. They're not letting me in on the rules, she mused, and found herself grateful. She didn't want to play. Making her excuses to no one in particular, Autumn slipped from the room to find her aunt.

Whatever tension she had felt evaporated the moment Autumn stepped into her aunt's room.

"Oh, Autumn." Aunt Tabby lifted her glasses from her nose and let them dangle from a chain around her neck. "I was just reading a letter from your mother. I'd forgotten it was here until this minute. She says by the time I read this, you'll be here. And here you are." Smiling, she patted Autumn's hand. "Debbie always was so clever. Did you enjoy your pot roast, dear?"

"It was lovely, Aunt Tabby, thank you."

"We'll have to have it once a week while you're with us." Autumn smiled and thought of how she liked spaghetti. Paul probably gets spaghetti on his visits, she mused. "I'll just make a note of that, else it'll slip right through my mind." Autumn recalled that Aunt Tabby's notes were famous for their ability to slip into another dimension, and felt more hopeful. "Where are my glasses?" Aunt Tabby murmured, puckering her impossibly smooth brow. Standing, she rummaged through her desk, lifting papers and peering under books. "They're never where you leave them."

Autumn lifted the dangling glasses from her aunt's bosom, then perched them on her nose. After blinking a moment, Aunt Tabby smiled in her vague fashion.

"Isn't that strange?" she commented. "They were here all along. You're just as clever as your mother."

Autumn couldn't resist giving her a bone-crushing hug. "Aunt Tabby, I adore you!"

"You always were such a sweet child." She patted Autumn's cheek, then moved away, leaving the scent of lavender and talc hanging in the air. "I hope you like your surprise."

"I'm sure I will."

"You haven't seen it yet?" Her small mouth pouted in thought. "No, I'm quite sure I haven't shown you yet, so you can't know if you like it. Did you and Miss Bond have a nice chat? Such a lovely lady. I believe she's in show business."

Autumn's smile was wry. There was no one, she thought, absolutely no one like Aunt Tabby. "Yes, I believe she is. I've always admired her."

"Oh, have you met before?" Aunt Tabby asked absently as she shuffled the papers on her desk back into her own particular order. "I suppose I'd better show you now while I have it on my mind.''

Autumn tried to keep up with her aunt's thought processes, but it had been a year since her last visit and she was rusty. ''Show me what, Aunt Tabby?''

''Oh now, it wouldn't be a surprise if I told you, would it?'' Playfully, she shook her finger under Autumn's nose. ''You'll just have to be patient and come along with me.'' With this, she bustled from the room.

Autumn followed, deducing they were again discussing the surprise. She had to shorten her gait to match her aunt's. Autumn usually moved in a loose-limbed stride, a result of leanness and lengthy legs, while her aunt scuttled unrhythmically. Like a rabbit, Autumn thought, that dashes out in the road then can't make up its mind which way to run. As they walked, Aunt Tabby muttered about bed linen. Autumn's thoughts drifted irresistibly to Lucas.

''Now, here we are.'' Aunt Tabby stopped. She gave the door an expectant smile. The door itself, Autumn recalled, led to a sitting room long since abandoned and converted into a storage room. It was a convenient place for cleaning supplies, as it adjoined the kitchen.

"Well," Aunt Tabby said, beaming, "what do you think?"

Searching for the right comment, Autumn realized the surprise must be inside. "Is my surprise in there, Aunt Tabby?"

"Yes, of course, how silly." She clucked her tongue. "You won't know what it is until I open the door."

With this indisputable logic, she did.

When the lights were switched on, Autumn stood stunned. Where she had expected to see mops, brooms and buckets was a fully equipped darkroom. Every detail, every piece of apparatus stood neat and orderly in front of her. Her voice had been left outside the door.

"Well, what do you think?" Aunt Tabby repeated. She moved around the room, stopping now and again to peer at bottles of developing fluid, tongs and trays. "It all looks so technical and scientific to me." The enlarger caused her to frown and tilt her head. "I'm sure I don't understand a thing about it."

"Oh, Aunt Tabby." Autumn's voice finally joined her body. "You shouldn't have."

"Oh dear, is something wrong with it? Nelson told me you developed your own film, and the company that brought in all these things assured me everything was proper. Of course..." Her voice wavered in doubt. "I really don't know a thing about it."

Her aunt looked so distressed, Autumn nearly wept with love. "No, Aunt Tabby, it's perfect. It's wonderful." She enveloped the small, soft body in her arms. "I meant that you shouldn't have done this for me. All the trouble and the expense."

"Oh, is that all?" Aunt Tabby interrupted. Her distress dissolved as she beamed around the room again. "Well, it was no trouble at all. These nice young men came in and did all the work. As for the expense, well..." She shrugged her rounded shoulders. "I'd rather see you enjoy my money now than after I'm dead."

Sometimes, Autumn thought, the fuzzy little brain shot straight through to sterling sense. "Aunt Tabby." She framed her aunt's face with her hands. "I've never had a more wonderful surprise. Thank you."

"You just have a good time with it." Aunt Tabby's cheeks grew rosy with pleasure when Autumn kissed them, and she eyed the chemicals and trays again. "I don't suppose you'll blow anything up."

Knowing this wasn't a pun, and that her aunt was concerned about explosions in her vague way, Autumn assured her she would not. Satisfied, Aunt Tabby then bustled off, leaving Autumn to explore on her own.

For more than an hour, Autumn lost herself in what she knew best. Photography, started as a hobby when she had been a child, had become both craft and profession. The chemicals and complicated equipment were no strangers to her. Here, in a darkroom, or with a camera in her hands, she knew exactly who she was and what she wanted. This was where she had learned control—the same control she knew she had to employ over her thoughts of Lucas. She was no longer a dewy-eyed girl, ready to follow the crook of a finger. She was a professional woman with a growing reputation in her field. She had to hang on to that now, as she had for three years. There was no going back to yesterday.

Pleasantly weary after rearranging the darkroom to her own preference, Autumn wandered into the kitchen to fix herself a solitary cup of tea. The moon was round and white with a thin cloud drifting over it. Unexpectedly, a shudder ran through her, quick and chilling. The odd feeling she had sensed several times that evening came back. She frowned. Imagination? Autumn knew herself well enough to admit she had her share. It was part of her art. But this was different.

Discovering Lucas at the inn had jolted her system, and her emotions had been strained. That, she decided, was all that was wrong. The tension she had felt earlier was her own tension; the strain, her own strain. Dumping the remaining tea into the sink, she decided that what she needed was a good night's sleep. No dreams, she ordered herself firmly. She'd had her fill of dreams three years before.

The house was quiet now. Moonlight filtered in, leaving the corners shadowed. The lounge was dark, but as she passed, Autumn heard muted voices. She hesitated a moment, thinking to stop and say goodnight, then she detected the subtle signs that told her this wasn't a conversation, but an argument. There was anger in the hushed, sexless voices. The undistinguishable words were quick, staccato and passionate. She walked by quickly, not wanting to overhear a private battle. A brief oath shot out, steeped in temper, elegant in French.

Climbing the stairs, Autumn smothered a grin. Jacques, she concluded, was probably losing patience with Lucas's artistic stubbornness. For entirely malicious reasons, she hoped the Frenchman gave him an earful.

It wasn't until she was halfway down the hall to her room that Autumn saw that she'd been wrong. Even Lucas McLean couldn't be two places at once. And he was definitely in this one. In the doorway of another room, Lucas was locked in a very involved embrace with Julia Bond.

Autumn knew how his arms would feel, how his mouth would taste. She remembered it all, completely, as if no years had come between to dull the sensations. She knew how his hand would trail up the back until he cupped around the neck. And that his fingers wouldn't be gentle. No, there were no gentle caresses from Lucas.

There was no need for her to worry about being seen. Both Lucas and Julia were totally focused on each other. Autumn was certain that the roof could have toppled over their heads, and they would have remained unmoving and entwined. The pain came back, hatefully, in full force.

Hurrying by, she gave vent to hideous and unwelcome jealousy by slamming her door.

Chapter Three

The forest was morning fresh. It held a tranquility that was full of tangy scents and bird song. To the east, the sky was filled with scuttling rags of white clouds. An optimist, Autumn put her hopes in them and ignored the dark, threatening sky in the west. Streaks of red still crowned the peaks of the mountains. Gently, the color faded to pink before it surrendered to blue.

The light was good, filtering through the white clouds and illuminating the forest. The leaves weren't full enough to interfere with the sun, only touching the limbs of trees with dots of green. Sometimes strong, the breeze bent branches and tugged at Autumn's hair. She could smell spring.

Wood violets popped out unexpectedly, the purple dramatic against the moss. She saw her first robin marching importantly on the ground, listening for worms. Squirrels scampered up trees, down trees and over the mulch of last year's leaves.

Autumn had intended to walk to the lake, hoping to catch a deer at early watering, but when her camera insisted on planting itself in front of her face again and again, she didn't resist. She ambled along, happy in the solitude and in tune with nature.

In New York, she never truly felt alone—lonely sometimes, but not solitary. The city intruded. Now, cocooned by mountains and trees, she realized how much she'd needed to feel alone. To recharge. Since leaving California and Lucas, Autumn hadn't permitted herself time alone. There had been a void that had to be filled, and she'd filled it with people, with work, with noise—anything that would keep her mind busy. She'd used the pace of the city. It had been necessary. Now, she wanted the pace of the mountains.

In the distance, the lake shimmered. Reflections of the surrounding mountains and trees were mirrored in the water, reversed and shadowy. There were no deer, but as she drew closer, Autumn noticed two figures circling the far side. The ridge where she stood was some fifty feet above the small valley which held the lake. The view was spectacular.

The lake itself stretched in a wide finger, about a hundred feet in length, forty in width. The breeze that caught at Autumn's hair where she strode didn't reach down to the water; its surface was clear and still. The opaque water gradually darkened towards the center, warning of dangerous depths.

Autumn forgot the people walking around the lake, her mind fully occupied with angles and depths of field and shutter speeds. The distance was too great for her to make them out even if she had been interested.

The sun continued its rise, and Autumn was content. She stopped only to change film. As she replaced the roll, she noted that the lake was now deserted. The light was wrong for the mood she wanted and, turning, she began her leisurely journey back to the inn.

This time, the stillness of the forest seemed different. The sun was brighter, but she felt an odd disquiet she hadn't experienced in the paler light of dawn. Foolishly, she looked back over her shoulder, then told herself she was an idiot. Who would be following her? And why? Yet the feeling persisted.

The serenity had vanished. Autumn forced herself to put aside an impulsive desire to run back to the inn where there would be people and coffee brewing. She wasn't a child to take flight at the thought of ogres or gnomes. To prove to herself that her fantasies hadn't affected her, she forced herself to stop and take the time to perfect a shot of a cooperative squirrel. A faint rustle of dead leaves came from behind her and terror brought her scrambling to her feet.

"Well, Cat, still attached to a camera?"

Blood pounding in her head, Autumn stared at Lucas. His hands were tucked comfortably into the pockets of his jeans as he stood directly in front of her. For a moment, she couldn't speak. The fear had been sharp and real.

"What do you mean by sneaking up behind me that way?" When it returned, her voice was furious. She was annoyed that she'd been foolish enough to be frightened, and angry that he'd been the one to frighten her. She pushed her hair back and glared at him.

"I see you've finally developed the temper to match your hair," he observed in a lazy voice. He crossed the slight distance between them and stood close. Autumn had also developed pride and refused to back away.

"It gets particularly nasty when someone spoils a shot." It was a simple matter to blame her reaction on his interference with her work. Not for a moment would she amuse him by confessing fear.

"You're a bit jumpy, Cat." The devil himself could take lessons on smiling from Lucas

McLean, she thought bitterly. "Do I make you nervous?"

His dark hair curled in a confused tangle around his lean face, and his eyes were dark and confident. It was the confidence, she told herself, that she cursed him for. "Don't flatter yourself," she tossed back. "I don't recall you ever being one for morning hikes, Lucas. Have you developed a love of nature?"

"I've always had a fondness for nature." He was studying her with deep, powerful eyes while his mouth curved into a smile. "I've always had a penchant for picnics."

The pain started, a dull ache in her stomach. She could remember the gritty feel of sand under her legs, the tart taste of wine on her tongue and the scent of the ocean everywhere. She forced her gaze to stay level with his. "I lost my taste for them." She turned in dismissal, but he fell into step beside her. "I'm not going straight back," she informed him. The chill in her voice would have discouraged anyone else. Stopping, she took an off-center picture of a blue jay.

"I'm in no hurry," he returned easily. "I've always enjoyed watching you work. It's fascinating how absorbed you become." He watched her back, and let his eyes run down the length of her hair. "I believe you could be snapping a charging rhino and not give an inch until you'd perfected the shot." There was a slight pause as she remained turned away from him. "I saw that photo you took of a burned-out tenement in New York. It was remarkable. Hard, clean and desperate."

Wary of the compliment, Autumn faced him. She knew Lucas wasn't generous with praise. Hard, clean and desperate, she thought. He had chosen the words perfectly. She didn't like discovering that his opinion still mattered. "Thank you." She turned back to focus on a grouping of trees. "Still having trouble with your book?"

"More than I'd anticipated," he muttered. Suddenly, he swooped her hair up into his hands. "I never could resist it, could I?" She continued to give her attention to the trees. Her answer was an absent shrug, but she squeezed her eyes tightly shut a moment. "I've never seen another woman with hair like yours. I've looked, God knows, but the shade is always wrong, or the texture or the length." There was a seductive quality in his voice. Autumn stiffened against it. "It's unique. A fiery waterfall in the sun, deep and vibrant spilling over a pillowcase."

"You always had a gift for description." She adjusted her lens without the vaguest idea of what she was doing. Her voice was detached, faintly bored, while she prayed for him to go. Instead, his grip tightened on her hair. In a swift move, he whirled her around and tore the camera from her hands.

"Damn it, don't use that tone with me. Don't turn your back on me. Don't ever turn your back on me."

She remembered the dark expression and uncertain temper well. There'd been a time when she would have dissolved when faced with them. But not anymore, she thought fleetingly. Not this time.

"I don't cringe at being sworn at these days, Lucas." She tossed her head, lifting her chin. "Why don't you save your attention for Julia? I don't want it."

"So." His smile was light and amused in a rapid-fire change. "It was you. No need to be jealous, Cat. The lady made the move, not I."

"Yes, I noticed your mad struggle for release." Even as she spoke, she regretted the words. Annoyed, Autumn pushed away, but was only caught closer. His scent teased her senses and reminded her of things she'd rather forget. "Listen, Lucas," she ground out slowly as both anger and longing rose inside her. "It took me six months to realize what a bastard you are, and I've had three years to cement that realization. I'm a big girl now, and not susceptible to your abundant charms. Now, take your hands off me and get lost."

"Learned to sink your teeth in, have you, Cat?" To her mounting fury, his expression was more amused than insulted. His eyes lowered to her mouth for a moment, lingered then lifted. "Not malleable anymore, but just as fascinating."

Because his words hurt more than she had thought possible, she hurled a stream of abuse at him.

His laughter cut off her torrent like a slap. Abandoning verbal protest, Autumn began to struggle with a wild, furious rage. Abruptly, he molded her against him. Tasting of punishment and possession, his mouth found hers. The heat was blinding.

The old, churning need fought its way to the surface. For three years she had starved, and now all that hunger spilled out in response. There was no hesitation as her arms found their way around his neck. Eager for more, her lips parted. His mouth was urgent and bruising. The pain was like heaven, and she begged for more. Her blood was flowing again. Lucas let his mouth roam over her face, then come back to hers with new demands. Autumn met them and fretted for more. Time flew backward, then forward again before he lifted his face.

His eyes were incredibly dark, opaque with a passion she recognized. For the first time she felt the faint throbbing where his hands gripped her and his hold eased to a caress. The taste of him lingered on her lips.

"It's still there, Cat," Lucas murmured. With easy familiarity, he combed his fingers through her hair. "Still there."

All at once, pain and humiliation coursed through her. She pulled away fiercely and swung out a hand. He caught her wrist and, frustrated, she drew back with her other hand. His reflexes were too sharp, and she was denied any satisfaction. With both wrists captured, she could only stand struggling, her breath ragged. Tears burned at her throat, but she refused to acknowledge them. He won't make me cry, she vowed fiercely. He won't see me cry again.

In silence, Lucas watched her battle for control. There was no sound in the forest but Autumn's own jerking breaths. When she could speak, her voice was hard and cold. "There's a difference between love and lust, Lucas. Even you should know one from the other. What's there now may be the same for you, but not for me. I loved you. I *loved* you." The words were an accusation in their repetition. His brows drew together as his gaze grew intense. "You took it all once—my love, my innocence, my pride—then you tossed them back in my face. You can't have them back. The first is dead, the second's gone and the third belongs to me."

For a moment, they both were still. Slowly, without taking his eyes from hers, Lucas released her wrists. He didn't speak, and his expression told her nothing. Refusing to run from him a second time, Autumn turned and walked away. Only when she was certain he wasn't following did she allow her tears their freedom. Her statements about pride and innocence had been true. But her love was far from dead. It was alive, and it hurt.

As the red bricks of the inn came into view, Autumn dashed the drops away. There would be no wallowing in what was over. Loving Lucas changed nothing, any more than it had changed anything three years before. But she'd changed. He wouldn't find her weeping, helpless and—as he had said himself—malleable.

Disillusionment had given her strength. He could still hurt her. She'd learned that quickly. But he could no longer manipulate her as he had once. Still, the encounter with him had left her shaken, and she wasn't pleased when Helen approached from a path to the right.

It was impossible, without being pointedly rude, for Autumn to veer off and avoid her. Instead, she fixed a smile on her face. When Helen turned her head, the livid bruise under her eye became noticeable. Autumn's smile faded into quick concern.

"What happened?" The bruise looked painful and aroused Autumn's sympathy.

"I walked into a branch." Helen gave a careless shrug as she lifted her fingers to stroke the mark. "I'll have to be more careful in the future."

Perhaps it was her turmoil over Lucas that made Autumn detect some hidden shade of meaning in those words, but Helen seemed to mean more than she said. Certainly the eyes which met Autumn's were as hot and angry as the bruise. And the mark itself, Autumn mused, looked more like the result of contact with a violent hand than with any stray branch. She pushed the thought aside. Who would have struck Helen? she asked herself. And why would she cover up the abuse? Her own carelessness made more sense.

"It looks nasty," Autumn commented as they began to walk toward the inn. "You'll have to do something about it. Aunt Tabby should have something to ease the soreness."

"Oh, I intend to do something about it," Helen muttered, then gave Autumn her sharp-eyed smile. "I know just the thing. Out early taking pictures?" she asked while Autumn tried to ignore the unease her words brought. "I've always found people more interesting subjects than trees. I'm especially fond of candid shots." She began to laugh at some private joke. It was the first time Autumn had heard her laugh, and she thought how suited the sound was to Helen's smile. They were both unpleasant.

"Were you down at the lake earlier?" Autumn recalled the two figures she had spotted. To her surprise, Helen's laughter stopped abruptly. Her eyes grew sharper.

"Did you see someone?"

"No," she began, confused by the harshness of the question. "Not exactly. I saw two people by the lake, but I was too far away to see who they were. I was taking pictures from the ridge."

"Taking pictures," Helen repeated. Her mouth pursed as if she were considering something carefully. She began to laugh again with a harsh burst of sound.

"Well, well, such good humor for such early risers." Julia drifted down the porch steps. Her brow lifted as she studied Helen's cheek. Autumn wondered if the actress's shudder was real or affected. "Good heavens, what have you done to yourself?"

Helen's amusement seemed to have passed. She gave Julia a quick scowl, then fingered the bruise again. "Walked into a branch," she muttered before she stalked up the steps and disappeared inside.

"A fist more likely," Julia commented, and smiled. With a shrug, she dismissed Helen and turned to Autumn. "The call of the wild beckoned to you, too? It seems everyone but me was tramping through forests and over mountains at the cold light of dawn. It's so difficult being sane when one is surrounded by insanity."

Autumn had to smile. Julia looked like a sunbeam. In direct contrast to her own rough jeans and jacket, Julia wore delicate pink slacks and a thin silk blouse flocked with roses. The white sandals she wore wouldn't last fifty yards in the woods. Whatever resentment Autumn had felt for the actress attracting Lucas vanished under her open warmth.

"There are some," Autumn remarked mildly, "who might accuse you of laziness."

"Absolutely," Julia agreed with a nod and a smile. "When I'm not working, I wallow in sloth. If I don't get going again soon, my blood will stop flowing." She gave Autumn a shrewd glance. "Looks like you walked into a rather large branch yourself."

Bewilderment crossed Autumn's face briefly. Julia's eyes, she discovered, were very discerning. The traces of tears hadn't evaporated as completely as Autumn would have liked. Helplessly she moved her shoulders. "I heal quickly."

"Brave child. Come, tell mama all about it." Julia's eyes were sympathetic, balancing the stinging lightness of the words. Linking her arms through Autumn's, she began to walk across the lawn.

"Julia..." Autumn shook her head. Inner feelings were private. She'd broken the rule for Lucas, and wasn't certain she could do so again.

"Autumn." The refusal was firmly interrupted. "You do need to talk. You might not think that you look stricken, but you do." Julia sighed with perfect finesse. "I really don't know why I've become so fond of you; it's totally against my policy. Beautiful women tend to avoid or dislike other beautiful women, especially younger ones."

The statement completely robbed Autumn of speech. The idea of the exquisite, incomparable Julia Bond placing herself on a physical plane anywhere near Autumn's own seemed ludicrous to her. It was one matter to hear the actress speak casually of her own beauty, and quite another for her to speak of Autumn's. Julia's voice flowed over the gaping silence.

"Maybe it's the exposure to those two other females—one so dull and the other so nasty— but I've developed an affection for you." The breeze tugged at her hair, lifting it up so that the sunlight streamed through it. Absently, Julia tucked a strand behind her ear. On the lobe a diamond sparkled. Autumn thought it incongruous that they were walking arm in arm among her aunt's struggling daffodils.

"You're also a kind person," Julia went on. "I don't know a great many kind people." She turned to Autumn so that her exquisite profile became her exquisite full face. "Autumn, darling, I always pry, but I also know how to keep a confidence."

"I'm still in love with him," Autumn blurted out, then followed that rash statement with a deep sigh. Before she knew it, words were tumbling out. She left out nothing, from the beginning to the end, to the new beginning when he had come back into her life the day before. She told Julia everything. Once she'd begun, no effort was needed. She didn't have to think, only feel, and Julia listened. The quality of her listening was so perfect, Autumn all but forgot she was there.

"The monster," Julia said, but with no malice. "You'll find all men, those marvelous creatures, are basically monsters."

Who was Autumn to argue with an expert? As they walked on in silence, she realized that she did feel better. The rawness was gone.

"The main trouble is, of course, that you're still mad about him. Not that I blame you," Julia added when Autumn made a small sound of distress. "Lucas is quite a man. I had a tiny sample last night, and I was impressed." Julia spoke so casually of the passion Autumn had witnessed, it was impossible to be angry. "Lucas is a talented man," Julia went on. By her smile, Autumn knew that Julia was very much aware of the struggle that was going on within Autumn. "He's also arrogant, selfish and used to being obeyed. It's easy for me to see that, because I am, too. We're alike. I doubt very much if we could even enjoy a pleasant affair. We'd be clawing at each other before the bed was turned down."

Autumn found no response to make to the image this produced, and merely walked on.

"Jacques is more my type," Julia mused. "But his attentions are committed elsewhere." She frowned, and Autumn sensed that her thoughts had drifted to something quite different. "Anyway." Julia made an impatient gesture. "You just have to make up your mind what you want. Obviously, Lucas wants you back, at least for as long as it suits him."

Autumn tried to ignore the sting of honesty and just listened.

"Knowing that, you could enjoy a stimulating relationship with him, with your eyes open."

"I can't do that, Julia. The knowing won't stop the hurting. I'm not sure I can survive another... relationship with Lucas. And he'd know I was still in love with him." A flash frame of their parting scene three years before jumped into her mind. "I won't be humiliated again. Pride's the only thing I have left that isn't his already."

"Love and pride don't belong together." Julia patted Autumn's hand. "Well then, you'll have to barricade yourself against the assault. I'll run interference for you."

"How will you do that?"

"Darling!" She lifted her brow as the slow, cat smile drifted to her lips.

Autumn had to laugh. It all seemed so absurd. She lifted her face to the sky. The black clouds were winning after all. For a moment, they blotted out the sun and warmth. "Looks like rain."

Her gaze shifted back to the inn. The windows were black and empty. The struggling light fell gloomily over the bricks and turned the white porch and shutters gray. Behind the building, the sky was like slate. The mountains were colorless and oppressive. She felt a tickle at the back of her neck. To her puzzlement, Autumn found she didn't want to go back inside.

Just as quickly, the clouds shifted, letting the sun pour out through the opening. The windows blinked with light. The shadows vanished. Chiding herself for another flight of fancy, Autumn walked back to the inn with Julia.

Only Jacques joined them for breakfast. Helen was nowhere in sight, and Steve and the Spicers were apparently still hiking. Autumn trained her thoughts away from Lucas. Her appetite, as usual, was unimpaired and outrageous. She put away a healthy portion of bacon, eggs, coffee and muffins while Julia nibbled on a single piece of thin toast and sent her envious scowls.

Jacques seemed preoccupied. His charm was costing him visible effort. Memory of the muffled argument in the lounge came to Autumn's mind. Idly, she began to speculate on who he had been annoyed with. Thinking it over, the entire matter struck her as odd. Jacques LeFarre didn't seem to be the sort of man who would argue with a veritable stranger, yet, as Autumn knew, both Lucas and Julia had been preoccupied elsewhere.

Appearing totally at ease, Julia rambled on about a mutual friend in the industry. But she's an actress, Autumn reminded herself. A good one. She could easily know the cause of last night's animosity and never show a sign. Jacques, however, wasn't an actor. The distress was there; anger lay just beneath the polished charm. Autumn wondered at it throughout the meal, then dismissed it from her mind as she left to find her aunt. After all, she reflected, it wasn't any of her business.

Aunt Tabby was, as Autumn had known she would be, fussing with Nancy the cook over the day's menu. Keeping silent, Autumn let the story unfold. It seemed that Nancy had planned on chicken while Aunt Tabby was certain they had decided on pork. While the argument raged, Autumn helped herself to another cup of coffee. Through the window, she could see the thick, roiling clouds continue their roll from the west.

"Oh, Autumn, did you have a nice walk?" When she turned, Autumn found her aunt smiling at her. "Such a nice morning, a shame it's going to rain. But that's good for the flowers, isn't it? Sweet little things. Did you sleep well?"

After a moment, Autumn decided to answer only the final question. There was no use confusing her aunt. "Wonderfully, Aunt Tabby. I always sleep well when I visit you."

"It's the air," the woman replied. Her round little face lit with pleasure. "I think I'll make my special chocolate cake for tonight. That should make up for the rain."

"Any hot coffee, Aunt Tabby?" Lucas swept into the kitchen as if he enjoyed the privilege daily. As always, when he came into a room, the air charged. This phenomenon Autumn could accept. The casual use of her aunt's nickname was more perplexing.

"Of course, dear, just help yourself." Aunt Tabby gestured vaguely toward the stove, her mind on chocolate cake. Autumn's confusion grew as Lucas strode directly to the proper cupboard, retrieved a cup and proceeded to fix himself a very homey cup of coffee.

He drank, leaning against the counter. The eyes that met Autumn's were very cool. All traces of anger and passion were gone, as if they had never existed. His rough black brows lifted as she continued to stare. The damnable devil smile tugged at his mouth.

"Oh, is that your camera, dear?" Aunt Tabby's voice broke into her thoughts. Autumn lowered her eyes.

The camera still hung around her neck, so much a part of her that she'd forgotten it was there.

"My, my, so many numbers. It looks complicated." Aunt Tabby peered at it through narrowed eyes, forgetting the glasses that dangled from her chain. "I have a very nice one, Autumn. You're welcome to use it whenever you like." After giving the Nikon another dubious glance, she beamed up with her misty smile. "You just push a little red button, and the picture pops right out. You can see if you've cut off someone's head or have your thumb in the corner right away, so you can take another picture. And you don't have to grope around in that darkroom either. I don't know how you see what you're doing in there." Her brows drew close, and she tapped a finger against her cheek. "I'm almost certain I can find it."

Autumn grinned. She was compelled to subject her aunt to yet another bear hug. Over the gray-streaked head, Autumn saw that Lucas was grinning as well. It was the warm, natural grin which came to his face so rarely. For a moment, she found she could smile back at him without pain.

Chapter Four

When the rain came, it didn't begin with the slow drip-drop of an April shower. As the sky grew hazy, the light in the lounge became dim. Everyone was back and the inn was again filled with its odd assortment of guests.

Steve, expanding on his role of bartender, had wandered to the kitchen to get coffee. Robert Spicer had trapped Jacques in what seemed to be a technical explanation of open-heart surgery. During the discussion, Julia sat beside him, hanging on every word—or seeming to. Autumn knew better. Occasionally, Julia sent messages across to her with her extraordinary eyes. She was enjoying herself immensely.

Jane sat sullen over a novel Autumn was certain was riddled with explicit sex. She wore dull brown again, slacks and a sweater. Helen, her bruise livid, smoked quietly in long, deep drags. She reminded Autumn eerily of Alice in Wonderland's caterpillar. Once or twice, Autumn found Helen's sharp eyes on her. The

speculative smile left her confused and uncomfortable.

Lucas wasn't there. He was upstairs, Autumn knew, hammering away at his type-
writer. She hoped it would keep him busy for
hours. Perhaps he'd even take his meals in his
room.

Abruptly, the dim light outdoors was snuffed
out, and the room plunged into gloom. The
warmth fled with it. Autumn shuddered with a
sharp premonition of dread. The feeling surprised her, as storms had always held a primitive appeal for her. For a heartbeat, there was
no sound, then the rain began with a gushing
explosion. With instant force, instant fury, it
battered against the windows, punctuated by
wicked flashes of lightning.

"A spring shower in the mountains," Steve
observed. He paused a moment in the doorway with a large tray balanced in his hands.
The friendly scent of coffee entered with him.

"More like special effects," Julia returned.
With a flutter of her lashes, she cuddled toward Robert. "Storms are so terrifying and
moving. I find myself longing to be frightened."

It was straight out of *A Long Summer's
Evening*, Autumn noted, amused. But the
doctor seemed too overcome with Julia's in-

genuous eyes to recognize the line. Autumn wanted to laugh badly. When Julia cuddled even closer and sent her a wink, Autumn's eyes retreated to the ceiling.

Jane wasn't amused. Autumn noticed she was no longer sullen but smoldering. Perhaps she had claws after all, Autumn thought, and felt she would like her better for it. It might be wise, she mused as Steve passed her a cup of coffee, if Julia concentrated on him rather than the doctor.

"Cream, no sugar, right?" Steve smiled down at her with his California blue eyes. Autumn's lips curved in response. He was a man with the rare ability to make a woman feel pampered without being patronizing. She admired him for it.

"Right. You've got a better memory than George." Her eyes smiled at him over the rim of her cup. "You serve with such style, too. Have you been in this line of work long?"

"I'm only here on a trial basis," he told her with a grin. "Please pass your comments on to the management."

Lightning speared through the gloom again. Jacques shifted in his seat as thunder rumbled and echoed through the room. "With such a storm, is it not possible to lose power?" he addressed Autumn.

"We often lose power." Her answer, accompanied by an absent shrug, brought on varying reactions.

Julia found the idea marvelous—candlelight was so wonderfully romantic. At the moment, Robert couldn't have agreed more. Jacques appeared not to care one way or the other. He lifted his hands in a Gallic gesture, indicating his acceptance of fate.

Steve and Helen seemed inordinately put out, though his comments were milder than hers. He mumbled once about inconveniences, then stalked over to the window to stare out at the torrent of wind and rain. Helen was livid.

"I didn't pay good money to grope around in the dark and eat cold meals." Lighting another cigarette with a swift, furious gesture, she glared at Autumn. "It's intolerable that we should have to put up with such inefficiency. Your aunt will certainly have to make the proper adjustments. I for one won't pay these ridiculous prices, then live like a pioneer." She waved her cigarette, preparing to continue, but Autumn cut her off. She aimed the cold, hard stare she had recently developed.

"I'm sure my aunt will give your complaints all the consideration they warrant." Turning pointedly away, she allowed Helen's sharp little darts to bounce off her. "Actually," she told Jacques, noting his smile of approval, "we have a generator. My uncle was as practical as Aunt Tabby is..."

"Charming," Steve supplied, and instantly became her friend.

After she'd finished beaming at him, Autumn continued. "If we lose main power, we switch over to the generator. With that, we can maintain essential power with little inconvenience."

"I believe I'll have candles in my room anyway," Julia decided. She gave Robert an under-the-lashes smile as he lit her cigarette.

"Julia should have been French," Jacques commented. His moustache tilted at the corner. "She's an incurable romantic."

"Too much...romance," Helen murmured, "can be unwise." Her eyes swept the room, then focused on Julia.

Before Autumn's astonished gaze, Julia transformed from mischievous angel to tough lady. "I've always found that only idiots think they're wise." Statement made, she melted back into a celestial being so quickly, Autumn blinked.

Seeing her perform on the screen was nothing compared to a live show. It occurred to Autumn that she had no inkling which woman was the real Julia Bond—if indeed she was either. The notion germinated that she really didn't know any of the people in that room. They were all strangers.

The air was still vibrating with the uncomfortable silence when Lucas entered. He seemed impervious to the swirling tension. Helplessly, Autumn's eyes locked on his. He came to her, ignoring the others in his cavalier fashion. The devil smile was on his face.

She felt a tremor when she couldn't stop the room from receding, leaving only him in her vision. Something of that fear must have been reflected in her face.

"I'm not going to eat you, Cat," Lucas murmured. Against the violent sounds of the storm, his voice was low, only for her. "Do you still like to walk in the rain?" The question was offhand, and didn't require an answer as he searched her face. "I remember when you did." He paused when she said nothing. "Your aunt sent you this." Lucas held out his hand, and Autumn's gaze dropped to it. Tension dissolved into laughter. "I haven't heard that in a long time," Lucas said softly.

She lifted her eyes to his again. He was studying her with a complete, singleminded intensity. "No?" As she accepted Aunt Tabby's famous red-button camera, her shoulders moved in a careless shrug. "Laughing's quite a habit of mine."

"Aunt Tabby says for you to have a good time with it." Dismissively, he turned his back on her and walked to the coffeepot.

"What have you got there, Autumn?" Julia demanded, her eyes following Lucas's progress.

Flourishing the camera, Autumn used a sober, didactic tone. "This, ladies and gentlemen, is the latest technological achievement in photography. At the mere touch of a button, friends and loved ones are beamed inside and spewed out onto a picture which develops before your astonished eyes. No focusing, no need to consult your light meter. The button is faster than the brain. Why, a child of five can operate it while riding his tricycle."

"It should be known," Lucas inserted in a dry voice, "that Autumn is a photographic snob." He stood by the window, carelessly drinking coffee while he spoke to the others. His eyes were on Autumn. "If it doesn't have interchangeable lenses and filters, multispeed shutters and impossibly complicated operations, it isn't a camera, but a toy."

"I've noticed her obsession," Julia agreed. She sent him a delicious look before she turned to Autumn. "She wears that black box like other women wear diamonds. She was actually tramping through the forest at the break of dawn, snapping pictures of chipmunks and bunnies.''

With a good-natured grin, Autumn lifted the camera and snapped Julia's lovely face.

"Really, darling," Julia said with a professional toss of the head. "You might have given me the chance to turn my best side."

"You haven't got a best side," Autumn countered.

Julia smiled, obviously torn between amusement and insult while Jacques exploded with laughter. "And I thought she was such a sweet child," she murmured.

"In my profession, Miss Bond," Autumn returned gravely, "I've had occasion to photograph a fair number of women. This one you shoot from the left profile, that one from the right, another straight on. Still another from an upward angle, and so on." Pausing a moment, she gave Julia's matchless face a quick, critical survey. "I could shoot you from any position, any angle, any light, and the result would be equally wonderful."

"Jacques." Julia placed a hand on his arm. "We really must adopt this girl. She's invaluable for my ego."

"Professional integrity," Autumn claimed before placing the quickly developing snapshot on the table. She aimed Aunt Tabby's prize at Steve.

"You should be warned that with a camera of any sort in her hands, Autumn becomes a dangerous weapon." Lucas moved closer. He lifted the snap of Julia and studied it.

Autumn frowned as she remembered the innumerable photographs she had taken of him. Under the pretext that they were art, she'd never disposed of them. She'd snapped and focused and crouched around him until, exasperated, he'd dislodged the camera from her hands and effectively driven photography from her mind.

Lucas saw the frown. With his eyes dark and unreadable, he reached down to tangle his fingers in her hair. "You never could teach me how to take a proper picture, could you, Cat?"

"No." The battle with the growing ache made her voice brittle. "I never taught you anything, Lucas. But I learned quite a bit."

"I've never been able to master anything but a one-button job myself." Steve ambled over. Autumn's camera sat on the table beside her. Picking it up, he examined it as if it were a strange contraption from the outer reaches of space. "How can you remember what all these numbers are for?"

When he perched on the arm of her chair, Autumn grasped at the diversion. She began a lesson in basic photography. Lucas wandered back to the coffeepot, obviously bored. From the corner of her eye, Autumn noticed Julia gliding to join him. Within moments, her hand was tucked into his arm, and he no longer appeared bored. Gritting her teeth, Autumn began to give Steve a more involved lesson.

Lucas and Julia left, arm in arm, ostensibly for Julia to nap and Lucas to work. Autumn's eyes betrayed her by following them.

When she dragged her attention back to Steve, she caught his sympathetic smile. That he understood her feelings was too obvious. Cursing herself, she resumed her explanations of f-stops, grateful that Steve picked up the conversation as if there had been no lull.

The afternoon wore on. It was a long, dreary day with rain beating against windows. Lightning and thunder came and went, but the wind built in force until it was one continuous moan. Robert tended the fire until flames crackled and spit. The cheery note this might have brought to the room was negated by Jane's sullenness and Helen's pacing. The air was tight.

Evading Steve's suggestion of cards, Autumn sought the peace and activity of her darkroom. As she closed and locked the door behind her, the headache which had started to build behind her temples eased.

This room was without tensions. Her senses picked up no nagging, intangible disturbances here, but were clear and ready to work. Step by step, she took her film through the first stages of development, preparing chemicals, checking temperatures, setting timers. Growing absorbed, she forgot the battering storm.

While it was necessary, Autumn worked in a total absence of light. Her fingers were her eyes at this stage and she worked quickly. Over the muffled sound of the storm, she heard a faint rattle. She ignored it, busy setting the timer for the next stage of developing. When the sound came again, it annoyed her.

Was it the doorknob? she wondered. Had she remembered to lock the door? All she needed at that point was for some layman to blunder in and bring damaging light with him.

"Leave the door alone," she called out just as the radio she had switched on for company went dead. There went the power, she concluded. Standing in the absolute darkness, Autumn sighed as the rattle came again.

Was it someone at the door, or just someone in the kitchen? Curious and annoyed, she walked in the direction of the door to make sure it was locked. Her steps were confident. She knew every inch of the room now. Suddenly, to her astonishment, pain exploded inside her head. Lights flashed and fractured before the darkness again became complete.

"Autumn, Autumn, open your eyes." Though the sound was far off and muffled, she heard the command in the tone. She resisted it. The nearer she came to consciousness, the more hideous grew the throbbing in her head. Oblivion was painless.

"Open your eyes." The voice was clearer now and more insistent. Autumn moaned.

Reluctantly, she opened her eyes as hands brushed the hair from her face. For a moment, she felt them linger against her cheek. Lucas came into focus gradually, dimming and receding until she forced him back, clear and sharp.

"Lucas?" Disoriented, Autumn could not think beyond his name. It seemed to satisfy him.

"That's better," he said with approval. Before any protest could be made, he kissed her hard, with a briefness that spoke of past intimacy. "You had me worried there a minute. What the hell did you do to yourself?"

The accusation was typical of him. She barely noticed it. "Do?" Autumn lifted a hand to touch the spot on her head where the pain was concentrated. "What happened?"

"That's my question, Cat. No, don't touch the lump." He caught her hand in his and held it. "It'll only hurt more if you do. I'm curious as to how you came by it, and why you were lying in a heap on the floor."

It was difficult to keep clear of the mists in her brain. Autumn tried to center in on the last thing she remembered. "How did you get in?" she demanded, remembering the rattling knob. "Hadn't I locked the door?" It came to her slowly that he was cradling her in his arms, holding her close against his chest. She struggled to sit up. "Were you rattling at the door?"

"Take it easy," he ordered as she groaned with the movement.

Autumn squeezed her eyes shut against the pounding in her head. "I must have walked into the door," she murmured, wondering at the quality of her clumsiness.

"You walked into the door and knocked yourself unconscious?" She couldn't tell if Lucas was angry or amused. The ache in her head kept her from caring one way or the other. "Strange, I don't recall you possessing that degree of uncoordination."

"It was dark," she grumbled, coherent enough to feel embarrassed. "If you hadn't been rattling around at the door..."

"I wasn't rattling around at your door," he began, but she cut him off with a startled gasp.

"The lights!" For a second time, she tried to struggle away from him. "You turned on the lights!"

"It was a mad impulse when I saw you crumpled on the floor," he returned dryly. Without any visible effort, he held her still. "I wanted to see the extent of the damage."

"My film!" Her glare was as accusing as her voice, but he responded with laughter.

"The woman's a maniac."

"Let go of me, will you?" Her anger made her less than gracious. Pushing away, she scrambled to her feet. At her movement, the pain grew to a crashing roar. She staggered under it.

"For God's sake, Autumn." Lucas rose and gripped her shoulders, steadying her. "Stop behaving like an imbecile over a few silly pictures."

This statement, under normal conditions, would have been unwise. In her present state of mind, it was a declaration of war. Pain was eclipsed by a pure silver streak of fury. She whirled on him.

"You never could see my work as anything but silly pictures, could you? You never saw me as anything but a silly child, diverting for awhile, but eventually boring. You always hated being bored, didn't you, Lucas?" She made a violent swipe at the hair that fell over her eyes. "You sit with your novels and bask in the adulation you get and look down your nose at the rest of us. You're not the only person in the world with talent, Lucas. My abilities are just as creative as yours, and my pictures give me as much fulfillment as your silly little books."

For a moment, he stood in silence, studying her with a frown. When he did speak, his voice was oddly weary. "All right, Autumn, now that you've gotten that out, you'd better get yourself some aspirin."

"Just leave me alone!" She shook off the hand he put on her arm. Turning, she started to take her camera from the shelf she had placed it on before beginning her work. Glancing down at the table, she flared again. "What do you mean by messing around with my equipment? You've exposed an entire roll of film!" Seething with fury, she whirled on him. "It isn't enough to interrupt my work by fooling around at the door, then turn on the lights and ruin what I've started. You have to put your hands into something you know nothing about.''

''I told you before, I wasn't fooling around at your door.'' His eyes were darkening dangerously. ''I came back after the power went out and the generator switched on. The door was open, and you were lying in a heap in the middle of the floor. I never touched your damned film.''

There was ice in his voice now to go with the heat in his eyes but Autumn was too infuriated to be touched by either. ''Foolish as it may seem,'' he continued, ''my concern and attention were on you.'' Moving toward her, he glanced down at the confusion on her work table. ''I don't suppose it occurred to you that in the dark you disturbed the film yourself?''

''Don't be absurd.'' Her professional ability was again insulted, but he cut off her retort in a voice filled with strained patience. Autumn pondered on it. As she remembered, Lucas had no patience at all.

''Autumn, I don't know what happened to your film. I didn't get any farther into the room than the spot where you were lying. I won't apologize for switching on the lights; I'd do precisely the same thing again.'' He circled her neck with his fingers and his words took on the old caressing note she remembered. "I happen to think your welfare is more important than your pictures."

Suddenly, her interest in the film waned. She wanted only to escape from him, and the feelings he aroused in her so effortlessly. Programmed response, she told herself. The soft voice and gentle hands tripped the release, and she went under.

"You're pale," Lucas muttered, abruptly dropping his hands and stuffing them into his pockets. "Dr. Spicer can take a look at you."

"No, I don't need—" She got no farther. He grabbed her arms with quicksilver fury.

"Damn it, Cat, must you argue with everything I say? Is there no getting past the hate you've built up for me?" He gave a quick shake. The pain rolled and spun in her head. For an instant, his face went out of focus as dizziness blurred her vision. Swearing with short, precise expertise, he pulled her close against him until the faintness passed. In a swift move, he lifted her into his arms. "You're pale as a ghost," he muttered. "Like it or not, you're going to see the doctor. You can vent your venom on him for a while."

By the time Autumn realized he was carrying her to her room, her temper had ebbed.

There was only a dull, wicked ache and the weariness. Flagging, she rested her head against his shoulder and surrendered. This wasn't the time to think about the darkroom door or how it had come to be opened. It wasn't the time to think of how she had managed to walk into it like a perfect fool. This wasn't the time to think at all.

Accepting the fact that she had no choice, Autumn closed her eyes and allowed Lucas to take over. She kept them closed when she felt him lower her to the bed, but she knew he stood looking down at her a moment. She knew too that he was frowning.

The sound of his footsteps told her that he had walked into the adjoining bathroom. The faint splash of water in the sink sounded like a waterfall to her throbbing head. In a moment, there was a cool cloth over the ache in her forehead. Opening her eyes, Autumn looked into his.

"Lie still," he ordered curtly. Lucas brooded down at her with an odd, enigmatic expression. "I'll get Spicer," he muttered abruptly. Turning on his heel, he strode to the door.

"Lucas." Autumn stopped him because the cool cloth had brought back memories of all the gentle things he had ever done. He'd had his gentle moments, though she'd tried hard to pretend he hadn't. It had seemed easier.

When he turned back, impatience was evident in the very air around him. What a man of contradictions he was, she mused. Intemperate, with barely any middle ground at all.

"Thank you," she said, ignoring his obvious desire to be gone. "I'm sorry I shouted at you. You're being very kind."

Lucas leaned against the door and stared back at her. "I've never been kind." His voice was weary again.

Autumn found it necessary to force back the urge to go to him, wipe away his lines of fatigue. He sensed her thoughts, and his eyes softened briefly. On his mouth moved one of his rare, disarming smiles.

"My God, Cat, you always were so incredibly sweet. So terrifyingly warm."

With that, he left her.

Chapter Five

Autumn was staring at the ceiling when Robert entered. Shifting her eyes, she looked at his black bag dubiously. She'd never cared for what doctors carried inside those innocent-looking satchels.

"A house call," she said and managed a smile. "The eighth wonder of the world. I didn't think you'd have your bag with you on vacation."

He was quick enough to note her uneasy glance. "Do you travel without your camera?"

"*Touché.*" She told herself to relax and not to be a baby.

"I don't think we'll need to operate." He sat on the bed and removed the cloth Lucas had placed there. "Mmm, that's going to be colorful. Is your vision blurred?"

"No."

His hands were surprisingly soft and gentle, reminding Autumn of her father's. She relaxed further and answered his questions on dizziness, nausea and so forth while watching his face. He was different, she noted. The competence was still there, but his dapper self-presentation had been replaced by a quiet compassion. His voice was kind, she thought, and so were his eyes. He was well suited to his profession.

"How'd you come by this, Autumn?" As he asked he reached in his bag and her attention switched to his hands. He removed cotton and a bottle, not the needle she'd worried about.

She wrinkled her nose ruefully. "I walked into a door."

He shook his head with a laugh, and began to bathe the bruise. "A likely story."

"And embarrassingly true. In the darkroom," she added. "I must have misjudged the distance."

His eyes shifted and studied hers a moment before they returned to her forehead. "You struck me as a woman who kept her eyes open," he said a bit grimly, Autumn thought, before he smiled again. "It's just a bump," he told her and held her hand. "Though my diagnosis won't make it hurt any less."

"It's only an agonizing ache now," Autumn returned, trying for lightness. "The cannons have stopped going off."

With a chuckle, he reached into his bag again. "We can do something about smaller artillery."

"Oh." She eyed the bottle of pills he held and frowned. "I was going to take some aspirin."

"You don't put a forest fire out with a water pistol." He smiled at her again and shook out two pills. "They're very mild, Autumn. Take these and rest for an hour or two. You can trust me," he added with exaggerated gravity as her brows stayed lowered. "Even though I am a surgeon."

"Okay." His eyes convinced her and she smiled back, accepting the glass of water and pills. "You're not going to take out my appendix or anything, are you?"

"Not on vacation." He waited until she had swallowed the medication, then pulled a light blanket over her. "Rest," he ordered and left her.

The next time Autumn opened her eyes, the room was in shadows. Rest? she thought and shifted under the blanket. I've been unconscious. How long? She listened. The storm was still raging, whipping against her windows with a fury she'd been oblivious to. Carefully, she pushed herself into a sitting position. Her head didn't pound, but a touch of her fingers assured her she hadn't dreamed up the entire incident. Her next thought was entirely physical—she discovered she was starving.

Rising, she took a quick glance in the mirror, decided she didn't like what she saw and went in search of food and company. She found them both in the dining room. Her timing was perfect.

"Autumn." It was Robert who spotted her first. "Feeling better?"

She hesitated a moment, embarrassed. Hunger was stronger, however, and the scent of Nancy's chicken was too tempting. "Much," she told him. She glanced at Lucas, but he said nothing, only watched her. The gentleness she had glimpsed so briefly before might have been an illusion. His eyes were dark and hard. "I'm starving," she confessed as she took her seat.

"Good sign. Any more pain?"

"Only in my pride." Forging ahead, she began to fill her plate. "Clumsiness isn't a talent I like to brag about, and walking into a door is such a tired cliché. I wish I'd come up with something more original."

"It's odd." Jacques twirled his fork by the stem as he studied her. "It doesn't seem to me that you would have the power enough to knock yourself unconscious."

"An amazon," Autumn explained and let the chicken rest for a delicious moment on her tongue.

"She eats like one," Julia commented. Autumn glanced over in time to catch the speculative look on her face before it vanished into a smile. "I gain weight watching her."

"Metabolism," Autumn claimed and took another forkful of chicken. "The real tragedy is that I lost the two rolls of film I shot on the trip from New York."

"Perhaps we're in for a series of accidents." Helen's voice was as hard as her eyes as they swept the table. "Things come in threes, don't they?" No one answered and she went on, fingering her own bruise. "It's hard to say what might happen next."

Autumn had come to detest the odd little silences that followed Helen's remarks, the fingers of tension that poked holes in the normalcy of the situation. On impulse, she broke her rule and started a conversation with Lucas.

"What would you do with this setting, Lucas?" She turned to him, but found no change in his expression. He's watching all of us, she thought. Just watching. Shaking off her unease, Autumn continued. "Nine people— ten really, counting the cook—isolated in a remote country inn, a storm raging. The main power's already snuffed out. The phone's likely to be next."

"The phone's already out," Steve told her. Autumn drew out a dramatic "Ah."

"And the ford, of course, is probably impassable." Robert winked at her, falling in with the theme.

"What more could you ask for?" Autumn demanded of Lucas. Lightning flashed, as if on cue.

"Murder." Lucas uttered the six-letter word casually, but it hung in the air as all eyes turned to him. Autumn shuddered involuntarily. It was the response she'd expected, yet she felt a chill on hearing it. "But, of course," he continued as the word still whispered in the air, "it's a rather overly obvious setting for my sort of work."

"Life is sometimes obvious, is it not?" Jacques stated. A small smile played on his mouth as he lifted his glass of golden-hued wine.

"I could be very effective," Julia mused. "Gliding down dark passageways in flowing white." She placed her elbows on the table, folded her hands and rested her chin on them. "The flame of my candle flickering into the shadows while the murderer waits with a silk scarf to cut off my life.''

"You'd make a lovely corpse," Autumn told her.

"Thank you, darling." She turned to Lucas. "I'd much rather remain among the living, at least until the final scene."

"You die so well." Steve grinned across the table at her. "I was impressed by your Lisa in *Hope Springs*."

"What sort of murder do you see, Lucas?" Steve was eating little, Autumn noted; he preferred the wine. "A crime of passion or revenge? The impulsive act of a discarded lover or the evil workings of a cool, calculating mind?"

"Aunt Tabby could sprinkle an exotic poison over the food and eliminate us one by one," Autumn suggested as she dipped into the mashed potatoes.

"Once someone's dead, they're no more use." Helen brought the group's attention back to her. "Murder is a waste. You gain more by keeping someone alive. Alive and vulnerable." She shot Lucas a look. "Don't you agree, Mr. McLean?"

Autumn didn't like the way she smiled at him. *Cool and calculating*. Jacques's words repeated in her mind. Yes, she mused, this was a cool and calculating woman. In the silence, Autumn shifted her gaze to Lucas.

His face held the faintly bored go-to-hell look she knew so well. "I don't think murder is always a waste." Again, his voice was casual, but Autumn, in tune with him, saw the change in his eyes. They weren't bored, but cold as ice. "The world would gain much by the elimination of some." He smiled, and it was deadly.

They no longer seemed to be speaking hypothetically. Shifting her gaze to Helen, Autumn saw the quick fear. *But it's just a game,* she told herself frantically and looked at Julia. The actress was smiling, but there was none of her summer warmth in it. She was enjoying watching Helen flutter like a moth on a pin. Noting Autumn's expression of dismayed shock, Julia changed the subject without a ripple.

After dinner, the group loitered in the lounge, but the storm, which continued unabated, was wearing on the nerves. Only Julia and Lucas seemed unaffected. Autumn noted how they huddled together in a corner, apparently enthralled with each other's company. Julia's laughter was low and rich over the sound of rain. Once, she watched Lucas pinch a strand of the pale hair between his fingers.

Autumn turned away. Julia ran interference expertly, and the knowledge depressed her.

The Spicers, without Julia as a distraction, sat together on the sofa nearest the fire. Though their voices were low, Autumn sensed the strain of a domestic quarrel. She moved farther out of earshot. A bad time, she decided, for Jane to confront Robert on his fascination with Julia when the actress was giving another man the benefit of her attentions. When they left, Jane's face was no longer sullen, but simply miserable. Julia never glanced in their direction, but leaned closer to Lucas and murmured something in his ear that made him laugh. Autumn found she, too, wanted out of the room.

It has nothing to do with Lucas, she told herself as she moved down the hall. I just want to say good night to Aunt Tabby. Julia's doing precisely what I want her to—keeping Lucas entertained. He never even looked at me once Julia stepped in between. Shaking off the hurt, Autumn opened the door to her aunt's room.

"Autumn, dear! Lucas told me you bumped your head." Aunt Tabby stopped clucking over her laundry list and rose to peer at the bruise. "Oh, poor thing. Do you want some aspirin? I have some somewhere."

Though she appreciated Lucas's consideration in giving her aunt a watered-down version, Autumn wondered at the ease of their relationship. It didn't seem quite in character for Lucas McLean to bother overmuch with a vague old woman whose claim to fame was a small inn and a way with chocolate cake.

"No, Aunt Tabby, I'm fine. I've already taken something."

"That's good." She patted Autumn's hand and frowned briefly at the bruise. "You'll have to be more careful, dear."

"I will. Aunt Tabby..."—Autumn poked idly at the papers on her aunt's desk—"how well do you know Lucas? I don't recall you ever calling a roomer by his first name." She knew there was no use in beating around the bush with her aunt. It would produce the same results as reading *War and Peace* in dim light—a headache and confusion.

"Oh, now that depends, Autumn. Yes, that really does depend." Aunt Tabby gently removed her papers from Autumn's reach before she focused on a spot in the ceiling. Autumn knew this meant she was thinking. "There's Mrs. Nollington. She has a corner room every September. I call her Frances and she calls me Tabitha. Such a nice woman. A widow from North Carolina."

"Lucas calls you Aunt Tabby," Autumn pointed out before her aunt could get going on Frances Nollington.

"Yes, dear, quite a number of people do. You do."

"Yes, but—"

"And Paul and Will," Aunt Tabby continued blithely. "And the little boy who brings the eggs. And . . . oh, several people. Yes, indeed, several people. Did you enjoy your dinner?"

"Yes, very much. Aunt Tabby," Autumn continued, determined that tenacity would prevail. "Lucas seems very much at home here."

"Oh, I am glad!" She beamed at her niece as she took Autumn's hand and patted it. "I do try so hard to make everyone feel at home. It always seems a shame to have to make them pay, but . . ." She glanced down at her laundry bills and began to mutter.

Give up, Autumn told herself. She kissed her aunt's cheek and left her to her towels and pillowcases.

It was growing late when Autumn finished putting her darkroom back in order. She left the door open this time and kept all the lights on. The echo of rain followed her inside as it beat on the kitchen windows. Other than its angry murmur, the house was silent.

No, Autumn thought, old houses are never silent. They creak and whisper, but the groaning boards and settling didn't disturb her. She liked the humming quality of the silence. Absorbed and content, she emptied trays and replaced bottles. She threw her ruined film into the wastecan with a sigh.

That hurts a bit, she thought, but there's nothing to be done about it. Tomorrow, she decided, she'd develop the film she'd taken that morning—the lake, the early sun, the mirrored trees. It would put her in a better frame of mind. Stretching her back, she lifted her hair from her neck, feeling pleasantly tired.

"I remember you doing that in the mornings."

Autumn whirled, her hair flying out from her shoulders as quick fear brought her heart to her throat. Pushing strands from her face, she stared at Lucas.

He leaned against the open doorway, a cup of coffee in his hand. His eyes locked on hers without effort.

"You'd pull up your hair, then let it fall, tumbling down your back until I ached to get my hands on it." His voice was deep and strangely raw. Autumn couldn't speak at all. "I often wondered if you did it on purpose, just to drive me mad." As he studied her face, he frowned, then lifted the coffee to his lips. "But, of course you didn't. I've never known anyone else who could arouse with such innocence."

"What are you doing here?" The trembling in her voice took some of the power out of the demand.

"Remembering."

Turning, she began to juggle bottles, jumbling them out of their carefully organized state. "You always were clever with words, Lucas." Cooler now that she wasn't facing him, she meticulously studied a bottle of stop bath. "I suppose you have to be in your profession."

"I'm not writing at the moment."

It was easier to deliberately misunderstand him. "Your book still giving trouble?" Turning, Autumn again noticed the signs of strain and fatigue on his face. Sympathy and love flared up, and she struggled to bank them down. His eyes were much too keen. "You might have more success if you'd get a good night's sleep." She gestured toward the cup in his hands. "Coffee's not going to help."

"Perhaps not." He drained the cup. "But it's wiser than bourbon."

"Sleep's better than both." She shrugged her shoulders carelessly. Lucas's habits were no longer her concern. "I'm going up." Autumn walked toward him, but he stayed where he was, barring the door. She pulled up sharply. They were alone. The ground floor was empty but for them and the sound of rain.

"Lucas." She sighed sharply, wanting him to think her impatient rather than vulnerable. "I'm tired. Don't be troublesome."

His eyes smoldered at her tone. Though Autumn remained calm, she could feel her knees turning to water. The dull, throbbing ache was back in her head. When he moved aside, she switched off the lights, then brushed past him. Swiftly, he took her arm, preventing what she had thought was going to be an easy exit.

"There'll come a time, Cat," he murmured, "when you won't walk away so easily."

"Don't threaten me with your overactive masculinity." Her temper rose and she forgot caution. "I'm immune now."

She was jerked against him. All she could see was his fury. "I've had enough of this."

His mouth took hers roughly; she could taste the infuriated desire. When she struggled, he pinned her back against the wall, holding her arms to her sides and battering at her will with his mouth alone. She could feel herself going under and hating herself for it as much, she told herself, as she hated him. His lips didn't soften, even when her struggles ceased. He took and took as the anger vibrated between them.

Her heart was thudding wildly, and she could feel the mad pace of his as they pressed together. Passion was all-encompassing, and her back was to the wall. There's no escape, she thought dimly. There's never been any escape from him. No place to run. No place to hide. She began to tremble with fear and desire.

Abruptly he pulled away. His eyes were so dark, she saw nothing but her own reflection. I'm lost in him, she thought. I've always been lost in him. Then he was shaking her, shocking a gasp out of her.

"Watch how far you push," he told her roughly. "Damn it, you'd better remember I haven't any scruples. I know how to deal with people who pick fights with me." He stopped, but his fingers still dug into her skin. "I'll take you, Cat, take you kicking and screaming if you push me much further."

Too frightened by the rage she saw in his face to think of pride, she twisted away. She flew down the hall and up the stairs.

Chapter Six

Autumn reached her door, out of breath and fighting tears. He shouldn't be allowed to do this to her. She couldn't allow it. Why had he barged back into her life this way? Just when she was beginning to get over him. *Liar.* The voice was clear as crystal inside her head. You've never gotten over him. Never. But I will. She balled her hands into fists as she stood outside her door and caught her breath. I will get over him.

Hearing the sound of his footsteps on the stairs, she fumbled with the doorknob. She didn't want to deal with him again tonight. Tomorrow was soon enough.

Something was wrong. Autumn knew it the moment she opened her door and stumbled into the dark. The scent of perfume was so strong, her head whirled with it. She groped for the light and when it flashed on, she gave a small sound of despair.

The drawers and closet had been turned out and her clothes were tossed and scattered across the room. Some were ripped and torn, others merely lay in heaps. Her jewelry had been dumped from its box and tossed indiscriminately over the mounds of clothes. Bottles of cologne and powder had been emptied out and flung everywhere. Everything—every small object or personal possession—had been abused or destroyed.

She stood frozen in shock and disbelief. The wrong room, she told herself dumbly. This had to be the wrong room. But the lawn print blouse with its sleeve torn at the shoulder had been a Christmas gift from Will. The sandals, flung into a corner and slashed, she had bought herself in a small shop off Fifth Avenue the summer before.

"No." She shook her head as if that would make it all go away. "It's not possible."

"Good God!" Lucas's voice came from behind her. Autumn turned to see him staring into her room.

"I don't understand." The words were foolish, but they were all she had. Slowly, Lucas shifted his attention to her face. She made a helpless gesture. "Why?"

He came to her, and with his thumb brushed a tear from her cheek. "I don't know, Cat. First we have to find out who."

"But it's—it's so spiteful." She wandered through the rubble of her things, still thinking she must be dreaming. "No one here would have any reason to do this to me. You'd have to hate someone to do this, wouldn't you? No one here has any reason to hate me. No one even knew me before last night."

"Except me."

"This isn't your style." She pressed her fingers to her temple and struggled to understand. "You'd find a more direct way of hurting me."

"Thanks."

Autumn looked over at him and frowned, hardly aware of what was being said. His expression was brooding as he studied her face. She turned away. She wasn't up to discussing Lucas McLean. Then she saw it.

"Oh, *no!*"

Scrambling on all fours, Autumn worked her way over the mangled clothes and began pushing at the tangled sheets of her bed. Her hands shook as she reached for her camera. The lens was shattered, with spiderweb cracks spreading over the surface. The back was broken, hanging drunkenly on one hinge. The film streamed out like the tail of a kite. Exposed. Ruined. The mirror was crushed. With a moan, she cradled it in her hands and began to weep.

Her clothes and trinkets meant nothing, but the Nikon was more to her than a single-reflex camera. It was as much a part of her as her hands. With it, she had taken her first professional picture. Its mutilation was rape.

Her face was suddenly buried against a hard chest. She made no protest as Lucas's arms came around her, but wept bitterly. He said nothing, offered no comforting words, but his hands were unexpectedly gentle, his arms strong.

"Oh, Lucas." She drew away from him with a sigh. "It's so senseless."

"There's sense to it somewhere, Cat. There always is."

She looked back up at him. "Is there?" His eyes were keeping their secrets so she dropped her own back to her mangled camera. "Well, if someone wanted to hurt me, this was the right way."

Her fingers clenched on the camera. She was suddenly, fiercely angry; it pushed despair and tears out of her mind. Her body flooded with it. She wasn't going to sit and weep any longer. She was going to do something. Pushing her camera into Lucas's hands, Autumn scrambled to her feet.

"Wait à minute." He grabbed her hand before she could rush from the room. "Where are you going?"

"To drag everyone out of bed," she snapped at him, jerking her hand. "And then I'm going to break someone's neck."

He didn't have an easy time subduing her. Ultimately, he pinned her by wrapping his arms around her and holding her against him. "You probably could." There was a touch of surprised admiration in his tone, but it brought her no pleasure.

"Watch me," she challenged.

"Calm down first." He tightened his grip as she squirmed against him.

"I want—"

"I know what you want, Cat, and I don't blame you. But you have to think before you rush in."

"I don't have anything to think about," she tossed back. "Someone's going to pay for this."

"All right, fair enough. Who?"

His logic annoyed her, but succeeded in taking her temper from boil to simmer. "I don't know yet." With an effort, she managed to take a deep breath.

"That's better." He smiled and kissed her lightly. "Though your eyes are still lethal enough." He loosened his grip, but kept a hold on her arm. "Just keep your claws sheathed, Cat, until we find out what's going on. Let's go knock on a few doors."

Julia's room adjoined hers, so Autumn steered there first. Her rage was now packed in ice. Systematic, she told herself, aware of Lucas's grip. All right, we'll be systematic until we find out who did it. And then...

She knocked sharply on Julia's door. After the second knock, Julia answered with a soft, husky slur.

"Get up, Julia," Autumn demanded. "I want to talk to you."

"Autumn, darling." Her voice evoked a picture of Julia snuggling into her pillows. "Even I require beauty sleep. Go away like a good girl."

"Up, Julia," Autumn repeated, barely restraining herself from shouting. "Now."

"Goodness, aren't we grumpy. I'm the one who's being dragged from my bed."

She opened the door, a vision in a white lace negligee, her hair a tousled halo around her face, her eyes dark and heavy with sleep.

"Well, I'm up." Julia gave Lucas a slow, sensual smile and ran a hand through her hair. "Are we going to have a party?"

"Someone tore my room apart," Autumn stated bluntly. She watched Julia's attention switch from the silent flirtation with Lucas to her.

"What?" The catlike expression had melted into a frown of concentration. An actress, Autumn reminded herself. She's an actress and don't forget it.

"My clothes were pulled out and ripped, tossed around the room. My camera's broken." She swallowed on this. It was the most difficult to accept.

"That's crazy." Julia was no longer leaning provocatively against the door, but standing straight. "Let me see." She brushed past them and hurried down the hall. Stopping in the doorway of Autumn's room, she stared. Her eyes, when they turned back, were wide with shock. "Autumn, how awful!" She came back and slipped an arm around Autumn's waist. "How perfectly awful. I'm so sorry."

Sincerity, sympathy, shock. They were all there. Autumn wanted badly to believe them.

"Who would have done that?" she demanded of Lucas. Autumn saw that Julia's eyes were angry now. She was again the tough lady Autumn had glimpsed briefly that afternoon.

"We intend to find out. We're going to wake the others." Something passed between them. Autumn saw it flash briefly, then it was gone.

"All right," Julia said. "Then let's do it." She pushed her hair impatiently behind her ears. "I'll get the Spicers, you get Jacques and Steve. You," she continued to Autumn, "wake up Helen."

Her tone carried enough authority that Autumn found herself turning down the hall to Helen's room. She could hear the pounding, the answering stirs and murmurs from behind her. Reaching Helen's door, Autumn banged against it. This, at least, she thought, was progress. Lucas was right. We need a trial before we can hang someone.

Her knock went unanswered. Annoyed, Autumn rapped again. She wasn't in the mood to be ignored. Now there was more activity behind her as people came out of their rooms to stare at the disaster in hers.

"Helen!" She knocked again with fraying patience. "Come out here." She pushed the door open. It would give her some satisfaction to drag at least one person from bed. Ruthlessly, she switched on the light. "Helen, I—"

Helen wasn't in bed. Autumn stared at her, too shocked to feel horror. She was on the floor, but she wasn't sleeping. She was done with sleeping. Was that blood? Autumn thought in dumb fascination. She took a step forward before the reality struck her.

Horror gripped her throat, denying her the release of screaming. Slowly, she backed away. It was a nightmare. Starting with her room, it was all a nightmare. None of it was real. Lucas's careless voice played back in her head. *Murder.* Autumn shook her head as she backed into a wall. No, that was only a game. She heard a voice shouting in terror for Lucas, not even aware it was her own. Then blessedly, her hands came up to cover her eyes.

"Get her out of here." Lucas's rough command floated through Autumn's brain. She was trapped in a fog of dizziness. Arms came round her and led her from the room.

"Oh my God." Steve's voice was unsteady. When Autumn found the strength to look up at him, his face was ashen. She struggled against the faintness and buried her face in his chest. When was she going to wake up?

Confusion reigned around her. She heard disembodied voices as she drifted from horror to shock. There were Julia's smoky tones, Jane's gravelly voice and Jacques's rapid French-English mixture. Then Lucas's voice joined in—calm, cool, like a splash of cold water.

"She's dead. Stabbed. The phone's out so I'm going into the village to get the police."

"Murdered? She was murdered? Oh God!" Jane's voice rose, then became muffled. Raising her head, Autumn saw Jane being held tightly against her husband.

"I think, as a precaution, Lucas, no one should leave the inn alone." Robert took a deep breath as he cradled his wife. "We have to face the implications."

"I'll go with him." Steve's voice was strained and uneven. "I could use the fresh air."

With a curt nod, Lucas focused on Autumn. His eyes never left hers as he spoke to Robert. "Have you got something to put her out? She can double up with Julia tonight."

"I'm fine." Autumn managed to speak as she drew back from Steve's chest. "I don't want anything." It wasn't a dream, but real, and she had to face it. "Don't worry about me, it's not me. I'm all right." Hysteria was bubbling, and she bit down on her lip to cut it off.

"Come on, darling." Julia's arm replaced Steve's. "We'll go downstairs and sit down for a while. She'll be all right."

"I want—"

"I said she'll be all right," Julia cut off Lucas's protest sharply. "I'll see to her. Do what you have to do." Before he could speak again, she led Autumn down the staircase.

"Sit down," she ordered, nudging Autumn onto the sofa. "You could use a drink."

Looking up, Autumn saw Julia's face hovering over hers. "You're pale," she said stupidly before the brandy burned her throat and brought the world into focus with a jolt.

"I'm not surprised," Julia murmured and sank down on the low table in front of Autumn. "Better?" she asked when Autumn lifted the snifter again.

"Yes, I think so." She took a deep breath and focused on Julia's eyes. "It's really happening, isn't it? She's really lying up there."

"It's happening." Julia drained her own brandy. Color seeped gradually into her cheeks. "The bitch finally pushed someone too far."

Stunned by the hardness of Julia's voice, Autumn could only stare. Calmly, Julia set down her glass.

"Listen." Her tone softened, but her eyes were still cold. "You're a strong lady, Autumn. You've had a shock, a bad one, but you won't fall apart."

"No." Autumn tried to believe it, then said with more strength, "No, I won't fall apart."

"This is a mess, and you have to face it."
Julia paused, then leaned closer. "One of us
killed her."

Part of her had known it, but the rest had
fought against the knowledge, blocking it out.
Now that it had been said in cool, simple terms,
there was no escape from it. Autumn nodded
again and swallowed the remaining brandy in
one gulp.

"She got what she deserved."

"Julia!" Jacques strode into the room. His
face was covered with horror and disapproval.

"Oh, Jacques, thank God. Give me one of
those horrible French cigarettes. Give one to
Autumn, too. She could use it."

"Julia." He obeyed her automatically. "You
musn't speak so now."

"I'm not a hypocrite." Julia drew deeply on
the cigarette, shuddered, then drew again. "I
detested her. The police will find out soon
enough why we all detested her."

"Nom de Dieu! How can you speak so
calmly of it?" Jacques exploded in a quick,
passionate rage Autumn hadn't thought him
capable of. "The woman is dead, murdered.
You didn't see the cruelty of it. I wish to God I
had not."

Autumn drew hard on her cigarette, trying to
block out the picture that flashed back into her

mind. She gasped and choked on the power of the smoke.

"Autumn, forgive me." Jacques's anger vanished as he sat down beside her and draped an arm over her shoulders. "I shouldn't have reminded you."

"No." She shook her head, then crushed out the cigarette. It wasn't going to help. "Julia's right. It has to be faced."

Robert entered, but his normally swinging stride was slow and dragging. "I gave Jane a sedative." With a sigh, he too made for the brandy. "It's going to be a long night."

The room grew silent. The rain, so much a part of the night, was no longer noticeable. Jacques paced the room, smoking continually while Robert kindled a fresh fire. The blaze, bright and crackling, brought no warmth. Autumn's skin remained chilled. In defense, she poured herself another brandy but found she couldn't drink it.

Julia remained seated. She smoked in long, slow puffs. The only outward sign of her agitation was the continual tapping of a pink-tipped nail against the arm of her chair. The tapping, the crackling, the hiss of rain, did nothing to diminish the overwhelming power of the silence.

When the front door opened with a click and a thud, all eyes flew toward the sound. Strings of tension tightened and threatened to snap. Autumn waited to see Lucas's face. It would be all right, somehow, as long as she could see his face.

"Couldn't get through the ford," he stated shortly as he came into the room. He peeled off a sopping jacket, then made for the community brandy.

"How bad is it?" Robert looked from Lucas to Steve, then back to Lucas. Already, the line of command had been formed.

"Bad enough to keep us here for a day or two," Lucas informed him. He swallowed a good dose of the brandy, then stared out the window. There was nothing to see but the reflection of the room behind him. "That's if the rain lets up by morning." Turning, he locked onto Autumn, making a long, thorough study. Again he had, in his way, pushed everyone from the room but the two of them.

"The phones," she blurted out, needing to say something, anything. "We could have phone service by tomorrow."

"Don't count on it." Lucas ran a hand through his dripping hair, showering the room with water. "According to the car radio, this little spring shower is the backlash of a tornado. The power's out all over this part of the state.'' He lit a cigarette with a shrug. ''We'll just have to wait and see.''

''Days.'' Steve flopped down beside Autumn, his face still gray. She gave him her unwanted brandy. ''It could be days.''

''Lovely.'' Rising, Julia went to Lucas. She plucked the cigarette from his fingers and drew on it. ''Well.'' She stared at him. ''What the hell do we do now?''

''First we lock and seal off Helen's room.'' Lucas lit another cigarette. His eyes stayed on Julia's. ''Then we get some sleep.''

Chapter Seven

Sometime during the first murky light of dawn, Autumn did sleep. She'd passed the night lying wide-eyed, listening to the sound of Julia's gentle breathing beside her. Though she'd envied her ability to sleep, Autumn had fought off the drowsiness. If she closed her eyes, she might see what she'd seen when she opened Helen's door. When her eyes did close, however, the sleep was dreamless—the total oblivion of exhaustion.

It might have been the silence that woke her. Suddenly, she found herself awake and sitting straight up in bed. Confused, she stared around her.

Julia's disorder greeted her. Silk scarves and gold chains were draped here and there. Elegant bottles cluttered the bureau. Small, incredibly high Italian heels littered the floor. Memory returned.

With a sigh, Autumn rose, feeling a bit ridiculous in Julia's black silk nightgown; it neither suited nor fit. After seeing herself in the mirror, Autumn was glad Julia had already awakened and gone. She didn't want to wear any of the clothes that might have survived the attack on her room, and prepared to change back into yesterday's shirt and jeans.

A note lay on them. The elegant, sloping print could only have been Julia's:

> Darling, help yourself to some undies and a blouse or sweater. I'm afraid my slacks won't fit you. You're built like a pencil. You don't wear a bra, and in any case, the idea of you filling one of mine is ridiculous.
>
> J.

Autumn laughed, as Julia had intended. It felt so good, so normal, that she laughed again. Julia had known exactly how I'd feel, Autumn realized, and a wave of gratitude swept through her for the simple gesture. She showered, letting the water beat hot against her.

Coming back to the bedroom, Autumn pulled out a pair of cobwebby panties. There was a stack of them in misted pastels that she estimated would cost as much as a wide-angle lens. She tugged on one of Julia's sweaters, then pushed it up to her elbows—it was almost there in any case. Leaving the room, she kept her eyes firmly away from Helen's door.

"Autumn, I was hoping you'd sleep longer."

She paused at the foot of the stairs and waited for Steve to reach her. His face was sleep shadowed and older than it had been the day before. A fragment of his boyish smile touched his lips for her, but his eyes didn't join in.

"You don't look as if you got much," he commented and lifted a finger to her cheek.

"I doubt any of us did."

He draped an arm over her shoulder. "At least the rain's slowed down."

"Oh." Realization slowly seeped in and Autumn gave a weak laugh. "I knew there was something different. The quiet woke me. Where is..." She hesitated as Lucas's name trembled on her tongue. "Everyone?" she amended.

"In the lounge," he told her, but steered her toward the dining room. "Breakfast first. I haven't eaten myself, and you can't afford to drop any weight."

"How charming of you to remind me." She managed a friendly grimace. If he could make the effort to be normal, so could she. "Let's eat in the kitchen, though."

Aunt Tabby was there, as usual, giving instructions to a much subdued Nancy. She turned as they entered, then enfolded Autumn in her soft, lavender-scented arms.

"Oh, Autumn, what a dreadful tragedy. I don't know what to make of it." Autumn squeezed her. Here was something solid to hold on to. "Lucas said someone killed the poor thing, but that doesn't seem possible, does it?" Drawing back, Aunt Tabby searched Autumn's face. "You didn't sleep well, dear. Only natural. Sit down and have your breakfast. It's the best thing to do."

Aunt Tabby could, Autumn mused, so surprisingly cut through to the quick when she needed to. She began to bustle around the room, murmuring to Nancy as Autumn and Steve sat at the small kitchen table.

There were simple, normal sounds and scents. Bacon, coffee, the quick sizzle of eggs. It was, Autumn had to agree, the best thing to do. The food, the routine, would bring some sense of order. And with the order, she'd be able to think clearly again.

Steve sat across from her, sipping coffee while she toyed with her eggs. She simply couldn't summon her usual appetite, and turned to conversation instead. The questions she asked Steve about himself were general and inane, but he picked up the effort and went with it. She realized, as she nibbled without interest on a piece of toast, that they were supporting each other.

Autumn discovered he was quite well traveled. He'd crisscrossed all over the country performing various tasks in his rôle as troubleshooter for his father's conglomerate. He treated wealth with the casual indifference of one who has always had it, but she sensed a knowledge and a dedication toward the company which had provided him with it. He spoke of his father with respect and admiration.

"He's sort of a symbol of success and ingenuity," Steve said, pushing his own half-eaten breakfast around his plate. "He worked his way up the proverbial ladder. He's tough." He grinned and shrugged. "He's earned it."

"How does he feel about you going into politics?"

"He's all for it." Steve glanced down at her plate and sent her a meaningful look. Autumn only smiled and shook her head. "Anyway, he's always encouraged me to 'go for what I want and I better be good at it.'" He grinned again. "He's tough, but since I am good at it and intend to keep it that way, we'll both be satisfied. I like paperwork." He gestured with both hands. "Organizing. Refining the system from within the system."

"That can't be as easy as it sounds," Autumn commented, encouraging his enthusiasm.

"No, but—" He shook his head. "Don't get me started. I'll make a speech." He finished off his second cup of coffee. "I'll be making enough of those when I get back to California and my campaign officially starts."

"It just occurs to me that you, Lucas, Julia and Jacques are all from California." Autumn pushed her hair behind her back and considered the oddity. "It's strange that so many people from the coast would be here at one time."

"The Spicers, too," Aunt Tabby added from across the room, deeply involved in positioning pies in the oven. "Yes, I'm almost sure Dr. Spicer told me they were from California. So warm and sunny there. Well"—she patted the range as if to give it the confidence it needed to handle her pies—"I must see to the rooms now. I moved you next door to Lucas, Autumn. Such a terrible thing about your clothes. I'll have them cleaned for you."

"I'll help you, Aunt Tabby." Pushing away her plate, Autumn rose.

"Oh no, dear, the cleaners will do it."

Smiling wasn't as difficult as Autumn had thought. "I meant with the rooms."

"Oh..." Aunt Tabby trailed off and clucked her tongue. "I do appreciate it, Autumn, I really do, but..." She looked up with a touch of distress in her eyes. "I have my own system, you see. You'd just confuse me. It's all done with numbers."

Leaving Autumn to digest this, she gave her an apologetic touch on the cheek and bustled out.

There seemed nothing to do but join the others in the lounge.

The rain, though it was little more than a mist now, seemed to Autumn like prison bars. Standing at the window in the lounge, she wished desperately for sun. Conversation did not sparkle. When anyone spoke, it was around or over or under Helen Easterman. Perhaps it would have been better if they'd closeted themselves in their rooms, but human nature had them bound together.

Julia and Lucas sat on the sofa, speaking occasionally in undertones. Autumn found his eyes on her too often. Her defenses were too low to deal with what one of his probing looks could do to her, so she kept her back to him and watched the rain.

"I really think it's time we talked about this," Julia announced suddenly.

"Julia." Jacques's voice was both strained and weary.

"We can't go on like this," Julia stated practically. "We'll all go crazy. Steve's wearing out the floor, Robert's running out of wood to fetch and if you smoke another cigarette, you'll keel over." Contrarily, she lit another herself. "Unless we want to pretend that Helen stabbed herself, we've got to deal with the fact that one of us killed her."

Into the penetrating silence, Lucas's voice flowed, calm and detached. "I think we can rule out suicide." He watched as Autumn pressed her forehead to the glass. "And conveniently, we all had the opportunity to do it. Ruling out Autumn and her aunt, that leaves the six of us."

Autumn turned from the window and found every eye in the room on her. "Why should I be ruled out?" She shuddered and lifted her arms to hug herself. "You said we all had the opportunity."

"Motive, Cat," he said simply. "You're the only one in the room without a motive."

"Motive?" It was becoming too much like one of his screenplays. She needed to cling to reality. "What possible motive could any of us have had?"

"Blackmail." Lucas lit a cigarette as she gaped at him. "Helen was a professional leech. She thought she had quite a little goldmine in the six of us." He glanced up and caught Autumn with one of his looks. "She miscalculated."

"Blackmail." Autumn could only mumble the word as she stared at him. "You're—you're making this up. This is just one of your scenarios."

He waited a beat, his eyes locked on hers. "No."

"How do you know so much?" Steve demanded. Slowly, Lucas's eyes swerved from Autumn. "If she were blackmailing you, it doesn't necessarily follow that she was blackmailing all of us."

"How clever of you, Lucas," Julia interjected, running a hand down his arm, then letting it rest on his. "I had no idea she was sticking her fangs in anyone other than the three of us." Glancing at Jacques, she gave him a careless shrug. "It seems we're in good company."

Autumn made a small sound, and Julia's attention drifted over to her. Her expression was both sympathetic and amused. "Don't look so shocked, darling. Most of us have things we don't particularly want made public. I might have paid her off if she'd threatened me with something more interesting." Leaning back, she pouted effectively. "An affair with a married senator..." She sent a lightning smile to Autumn. "I believe I mentioned him before. That hardly had me quaking in my shoes at the thought of exposure. I'm not squeamish about my indiscretions. I told her to go to hell. Of course," she added, smiling slowly, "there's only my word for that, isn't there?"

"Julia, don't make jokes." Jacques lifted a hand to rub his eyes.

"I'm sorry." Julia rose to perch on the arm of his chair. Her hand slipped to his shoulder.

"This is crazy." Unable to comprehend what was happening, Autumn searched the faces that surrounded her. They were strangers again, holding secrets. "What are you all doing here? Why did you come?"

"It's very simple." Lucas rose and crossed over to her, but unlike Julia, he didn't touch to comfort. "I made plans to come here for my own reasons. Helen found out. She was very good at finding things out—too good. She learned that Julia and Jacques were to join me." He turned, half blocking Autumn from the rest with his body. Was it protection, she wondered, or defense? "She must have contacted the rest of you, and made arrangements to have all her...clients here at once.''

"You seem to know quite a bit,'' Robert muttered. He poked unnecessarily at the fire.

"It isn't difficult to figure out,'' Lucas returned. ''I knew she was holding nasty little threats over three of us; we'd discussed it. When I noticed her attention to Anderson, and you and your wife, I knew she was sucking elsewhere, too.''

Jane began to cry in dry, harsh sobs that racked her body. Instinctively, Autumn moved past Lucas to offer comfort. Before she was halfway across the room, Jane stopped her with a look that was like a fist to the jaw.

"You could have done it just as easily as anyone else. You've been spying on us, taking that camera everywhere.'' Jane's voice rose dramatically as Autumn froze. ''You were working for her, you could have done it. You can't prove you didn't. I was with Robert.'' There was nothing bland or dull about her now. Her eyes were wild. ''I was with Robert. He'll tell you.''

Robert's arm came around her. His voice was quiet and soothing as she sobbed against his chest. Autumn didn't move. There seemed no place to go.

"She was going to tell you I was gambling again, tell you about all the money I'd lost." She clung to him, a sad sight in a dirt-brown dress. Robert continued to murmur and stroke her hair. "But I told you last night, I told you myself. I couldn't pay her anymore, and I told you. I didn't kill her, Robert. Tell them I didn't kill her."

"Of course you didn't, Jane. Everyone knows that. Come with me now, you're tired. We'll go upstairs."

He was leading her across the room as he spoke. His eyes met Autumn's half in apology, half in a plea for understanding. She saw, quite suddenly, that he loved his wife very much.

Autumn turned away, humiliated for Jane, sorry for Robert. The faint trembling in her hands indicated she'd been dealt one more shock. When Steve's arm came around her, she turned into it and drew the comfort offered.

"I think we could all use a drink," Julia announced. Moving to the bar, she poured a hefty glass of sherry, then took it to Autumn. "You first," she ordered, pressing the glass into her hand. "Autumn seems to be getting the worst of this. Hardly seems fair, does it, Lucas?" Her eyes lifted to his and held briefly before she turned back to the bar. He made no answer.

"She's probably the only one of us here who's even remotely sorry that Helen's dead."

Autumn drank, wishing the liquor would soften the words.

"She was a vulture," Jacques murmured. Autumn saw the message pass between him and Julia. "But even a vulture doesn't deserve to be murdered." Leaning back, he accepted the glass Julia brought him. He clasped her hand as she once again sat on the arm of his chair.

"Perhaps my motive is the strongest," Jacques said and drank once, deeply. "When the police come, all will be opened and studied. Like something under a microscope." He looked at Autumn, as if to direct his explanation to her. "She threatened the happiness of the two things most important to me—the woman I love and my children." Autumn's eyes skipped quickly to Julia's. "The information she had on my relationship with this woman could have damaged my suit for custody. The beauty of that love meant nothing to Helen. She would turn it into something sordid and ugly."

Autumn cradled her drink in both hands. She wanted to tell Jacques to stop, that she didn't want to hear, didn't want to be involved. But it was too late. She was already involved.

"I was furious when she arrived here with her smug smile and evil eyes." He looked down into his glass. "There were times, many times, I wanted my hands around her throat, wanted to bruise her face as someone else had done."

"Yes, I wonder who." Julia caught her bottom lip between her teeth in thought. "Whoever did that was angry, perhaps angry enough to kill." Her eyes swept up, across Steve and Autumn and Lucas.

"You were at the inn that morning," Autumn stated. Her voice sounded odd, thready, and she swallowed.

"So I was." Julia smiled at her. "Or so I said. Being alone in bed is hardly an airtight alibi. No..." She leaned back on the wing of the chair. "I think the police will want to know who socked Helen. You came in with her, Autumn. Did you see anyone?"

"No." Her eyes flew instantly to Lucas. His were dark, already locked on her face. There were warning signals of anger and impatience she could read too easily. She dropped her gaze to her drink. "No, I..." How could she say it? How could she think it?

"Autumn's had enough for a while." Steve tightened his arm protectively around her.

"Our problems don't concern her. She doesn't deserve to be in the middle."

"Poor child." Jacques studied her pale, strained face. "You've walked into a viper's nest, *oui?* Go sleep, forget us for a while."

"Come on, Autumn, I'll take you up." Steve slipped the glass from her hand and set it on the table. With one final glance at Lucas, Autumn went with him.

Chapter Eight

They didn't speak as they mounted the steps. Autumn was too busy trying to force the numbness from her brain. She hadn't been able to fully absorb everything she'd been told. Steve hurried her by Helen's door before stopping at the one beside Lucas's.

"Is this the room your aunt meant?"

"Yes." She lifted both hands to her hair, pushing its weight away from her face. "Steve." She searched his face and found herself faltering. "Is all this true? Everything Lucas said? Was Helen really blackmailing all of you?" She noted the discomfort in his eyes and shook her head. "I don't mean to pry, but—"

"No," he cut her off, then let out a long breath. "No, it's hardly prying at this point. You're not involved, but you're caught, aren't you?"

The word was so apt, so close to her own thinking, that she nearly laughed. Caught. Yes, that was it exactly.

"It seems McLean is right on target. Helen had information concerning a deal I made for the company—perfectly within the circle of the law, but ..." He gave a rueful smile and lifted his shoulders. "Maybe not quite as perfectly as it should have been. There was an ethical question, and it wouldn't look so good on paper. The technicalities are too complicated to explain, but the gist of it is I didn't want any shadows on my career. These days, when you're heading into politics, you have to cover all the angles."

"Angles," Autumn repeated and pressed her fingers to her temple. "Yes, I suppose you do."

"She threatened me, Autumn, and I didn't care for it—but it wasn't enough to provoke murder." He drew a quick breath and shook his head. "But that doesn't help much, does it? None of us are likely to admit it."

"I appreciate you telling me anyway," Autumn said. Steve's eyes were gentle on her face, but the lines and strain of tension still showed. "It can't be pleasant for you to have to explain."

"I'll have to explain to the police before long," he said grimly, then noted her expression. "I don't mind telling you, Autumn, if you feel better knowing. Julia's right." His fingers strayed absently to her hair. "It's much healthier to get it out in the open. But you've had enough for now." He smiled at her, then realized his hands were in her hair. "I suppose you're used to this. Your hair's not easy to resist. I've wanted to touch it since the first time I saw it. Do you mind?"

"No." She wasn't surprised to find herself in his arms, his mouth on hers. It was an easy kiss, one that comforted rather than stirred. Autumn relaxed with it, and gave back what she could.

"You'll get some rest?" Steve murmured, holding her to his chest a moment.

"Yes. Yes, I will. Thank you." She pulled back to look up at him, but her eyes were drawn past him. Lucas stood at the doorway of his room, watching them both. Without speaking, he disappeared inside.

When she was alone, Autumn lay down on the white heirloom bedspread, but sleep wouldn't come. Her mind ached with fatigue. Her body was numb from it, but sleep, like a spiteful lover, stayed away. Time drifted as her thoughts ran over each member of the group.

She could feel nothing but sympathy for Jacques and the Spicers. She remembered the Frenchman's eyes when he spoke of his children and could still see Robert protecting his wife as she sobbed. Julia, on the other hand, needed no sympathy. Autumn felt certain the actress could take care of herself; she'd need no supporting arm or soothing words. Steve had also seemed more annoyed than upset by Helen's threats. He, too, could handle himself, she felt. There was a streak of street sense under the California gloss; he didn't need Autumn to worry for him.

Lucas was a different matter. Though he had nudged admissions from the rest of them, whatever threat Helen had held over him was still his secret. He had seemed very cool, very composed when he'd spoken of blackmail—but Autumn knew him. He was fully capable of concealing his emotions when there was a purpose to it. He was a hard man. Who knew better than she?

Cruel? Yes, she mused. Lucas could be cruel. She still had the scars attesting to it. But murder? No. Autumn couldn't picture Lucas plunging something sharp into Helen Easterman. Scissors, she remembered, though she tried hard not to. The scissors that had lain on the floor beside Helen. No, she couldn't believe him capable of that. She wouldn't believe him capable of it.

Neither could she rationally believe it of any of the others. Could they all conceal such hate, such ugliness behind their shocked faces and shadowed eyes?

But, of course, one of them was the killer.

Autumn blanked it from her mind. She couldn't think of it anymore. Not just then. Steve's prescription was valid—she needed to rest. Yet she rose and walked to the window to stare out at the slow, hateful rain.

The knock at her door vibrated like an explosion. Whirling, she wrapped her arms protectively around her body. Her heart pounded while her throat dried up with fear. Stop it! she ordered herself. No one has any cause to hurt you.

"Yes, come in." The calmness of her own voice brought her relief. She was hanging on.

Robert entered. He looked so horribly weary and stricken, Autumn automatically reached out to him. She thought no more of fear. He clasped her hands and squeezed once, hard.

"You need food," he stated as he searched her face. "It shows in the face first."

"Yes, I know. My delicate hollows become craters very quickly." She made her own search. "You could use some yourself."

He sighed. "I believe you're one of those rare creatures who is inherently kind. I apologize for my wife."

"No, don't." His sigh had been long and broken. "She didn't mean it. We're all upset. This is a nightmare."

"She's been under a lot of strain. Before..." He broke off and shook his head. "She's sleeping now. Your head"—he brushed the hair from her forehead to examine the colorful bruise—"is it giving you any trouble?"

"No, none. I'm fine." The mishap seemed like some ridiculous comic relief in the midst of a melodrama now. "Can I help you, Robert?"

His eyes met hers, once, desperately, then moved away. "That woman put Jane through hell. If I'd just known, I would have put a stop to it long ago." Anger overpowered his weariness and he turned to prowl the room. "She tormented her, drained every drop of money Jane could raise. She played on a sickness, encouraging Jane to gamble to meet the payments. I knew nothing about it! I should have. Yesterday, Jane told me herself and I was going to enjoy dealing with the Easterman woman this morning." Autumn saw the soft, gentle hands clench into fists. "God help me, that's the only reason I'm sorry she's dead."

"Robert..." She wasn't certain what to say, how to deal with this side of his character. "Anyone would feel the same way," she said carefully. "She was an evil woman. She hurt someone you love." Autumn watched the fingers in his left hand relax, one at a time. "It isn't kind, but none of us will mourn her. Perhaps no one will. I think that's very sad."

He turned back and focused on her again. After a moment, he seemed to pull himself back under control. "I'm sorry you're caught up in this." With the anger gone from his eyes, they were vulnerable. "I'm going to go check on Jane. Will you be all right?"

"Yes."

She watched him go, then sank down into a chair. Each different crisis drained her. If possible, she was wearier now than before. When did the madness start? Only a few days ago she'd been safe in her apartment in Manhattan. She'd never met any of these people who were tugging at her now. Except one.

Even as she thought of him, Lucas strode in through the door. He stalked over to her, stared down and frowned.

"You need to eat," he said abruptly. Autumn thought of how tired she was of hearing that diagnosis. "I've been watching the pounds drop off you all day. You're already too thin."

"I adore flattery." His arrogant entrance and words boosted her flagging energy. She didn't have to take abuse from Lucas McLean anymore. "Don't you know how to knock?"

"I've always appreciated the understated-ness of your body, Cat. You remember." He pulled her to her feet, then molded her against him. Her eyes flashed with quick temper. "Anderson seems to have discovered the charm as well. Did it occur to you that you might have been kissing a murderer?"

He spoke softly while his hand caressed her back. His eyes were mocking her. Her temper snapped at the strain of fighting her need for him.

"One might be holding me now."

He tightened his fingers on her hair so that she cried out in surprise. The mockery was replaced by a burning, terrifying rage. "You'd like to believe that, wouldn't you? You'd like to see me languishing in prison or, better yet, dangling from the end of a rope." She would have shaken her head, but his grip on her hair made movement impossible. "Would that be suitable punishment for my rejecting you, Cat? How deep is the hate? Deep enough to pull the lever yourself?"

"No, Lucas. Please, I didn't mean—"

"The hell you didn't." He cut off her protest. "The thought of me with blood on my hands comes easily to you. You can cast me in the role of murderer, can't you? Standing over Helen with the scissors in my hand."

"No!" In defense, she closed her eyes. "Stop it! Please stop it." He was hurting her now, but not with his hands. The words cut deeper.

He lowered his voice in a swift change of mood. Ice ran down Autumn's back. "I could have used my hands and been more tidy." A strong, lean-fingered hand closed around her throat. Her eyes flew open.

"Lucas—"

"Very simple and no mess," he went on, watching her eyes widen. "Quick enough, too, if you know what to do. More my style. More—as you put it—direct. Isn't that right?"

"You're only doing this to frighten me." Her breath was trembling in and out of her lungs. It was as if he were forcing her to think the worst of him, wanting her to think him capable of something monstrous. She'd never seen him like this. His eyes were black with fury while his voice was cold, so cold. She shivered. "I want you to leave, Lucas. Leave right now."

"Leave?" He slid his hand from her throat to the back of her neck. "I don't think so, Cat." His face inched closer. "If I'm going to hang for murder, I'd best take what consolation I can while I have the chance."

His mouth closed fast over hers. She struggled against him, more frightened than she'd been when she'd turned on the light in Helen's room. She could only moan; movement was impossible when he held her this close. He slipped a hand under her sweater to claim her breast with the swift expertise of experience. Heart thudded madly against heart.

"How can anyone so skinny be so soft?" he murmured against her mouth. The words he'd spoken so often in the past brought more agony than she could bear. The hunger from him was thunderous; he was like a man who had finally broken free of his tether. "My God, how I want you." The words were torn from him as he ravaged her neck. "I'll be damned if I'll wait any longer."

They sank onto the bed. With all the strength that remained, she flailed out against him. Pinning her arms to her sides, Lucas stared down at her with a wild kind of fury. "Bite and scratch all you want, Cat. I've reached my limit."

"I'll scream, Lucas." The words shuddered out of her. "If you touch me again, I'll scream."

"No, you won't."

His mouth was on hers, proving him right and her wrong. His body molded to hers with bittersweet accuracy. She arched once in defense, in desperation, but his hands were roaming, finding all the secret places he'd discovered over three years before. There was no resisting him. The wild, reckless demand that had always flavored his lovemaking left her weak. He knew too much of her. Autumn knew, before his fingers reached the snap of her jeans, that she couldn't prevent her struggles from becoming demands. When his mouth left hers to roam her neck, she didn't scream, but moaned with the need he had always incited in her.

He was going to win again, and she would do nothing to stop him. Tears welled, then spilled from her eyes as she knew he'd soon discover her pitiful, abiding love. Even her pride, it seemed, again belonged to him.

Lucas stopped abruptly. All movement ceased when he drew back his head to stare down at her. She thought, through her blurred vision, that she saw some flash of pain cross his face before it became still and emotionless. Lifting a hand, he caught a teardrop on his fingertip. With a swift oath, he lifted his weight from her.

"No, I won't be responsible for this again." Turning, he stalked to the window and stared out.

Sitting up, Autumn lowered her face to her knees and fought against the tears. She'd promised herself he'd never see her cry again. Not over him. Never over him. The silence stretched on for what seemed an eternity.

"I won't touch you like this again," he said quietly. "You have my word, for what it's worth."

Autumn thought she heard him sigh, long and deep, before his footsteps crossed to her. She didn't look up, but only squeezed her eyes closed.

"Autumn, I...oh, sweet God." He touched her arm, but she only curled herself tighter into a ball in defense.

The room fell silent again. The dripping rain seemed to echo into it. When Lucas spoke again, his voice was harsh and strained. "When you've rested, get something to eat. I'll have your aunt send up a tray if you're not down for dinner. I'll see that no one disturbs you."

She heard him leave, heard the quiet click of her door. Alone, she kept curled in her ball as she lay down. Ultimately, the storm of tears induced sleep.

Chapter Nine

It was dark when Autumn awoke, but she was not refreshed. The sleep had been only a temporary relief. Nothing had changed while she had slept. But no, she thought as she glanced around the room. She was wrong. Something had changed. It was quiet. Really quiet. Rising, she walked to the window. She could see the moon and a light scattering of stars. The rain had stopped.

In the dim light, she moved to the bathroom and washed her face. She wasn't certain she had the courage to look in the mirror. She let the cold cloth rest against her eyes for a long time, hoping the swelling wasn't as bad as it felt. She felt something else as well. Hunger. It was a healthy sign, she decided. A normal sign. The rain had stopped and the nightmare was going to end. And now she was going to eat.

Her bare feet didn't disturb the silence that hung over the inn. She was glad of it. She wanted food now, not company. But when she passed the lounge, she heard the murmur of voices. She wasn't alone after all. Julia and Jacques were silhouetted by the window. Their conversation was low and urgent. Before she could melt back into the shadows, Julia turned and spotted her. The conversation ceased abruptly.

"Oh, Autumn, you've surfaced. We thought we'd seen the last of you until morning." She glided to her, then slipped a friendly arm around her waist. "Lucas wanted to send up a tray, but Robert outranked him. Doctor's orders were to let you sleep until you woke up. You must be famished. Let's see what your Aunt Tabby left for you."

Julia was doing all the talking, and quite purposefully leading Autumn away. A glance showed her that Jacques was still standing by the window, unmoving. Autumn let it go, too hungry to object.

"Sit down, darling," Julia ordered as she steered Autumn into the kitchen. "I'm going to fix you a feast."

"Julia, you don't have to fix me anything. I appreciate it, but—"

"Now let me play mother," Julia interrupted, pressing down on Autumn's shoulder until she sat. "You're past the sticky-finger stage, so I really quite enjoy it."

Sitting back, Autumn managed a smile. "You're not going to tell me you can cook."

Julia aimed an arched glance. "I don't suppose you should eat anything too heavy at this time of night," she said mildly. "There's some marvelous soup left from dinner, and I'll fix you my specialty. A cheese omelette."

Autumn decided that watching Julia Bond bustle around a kitchen was worth the market price of an ounce of gold. She seemed competent enough and kept up a bouncy conversation that took no brainpower to follow. With a flourish, she plopped a glass of milk in front of Autumn.

"I'm not really very fond of milk," Autumn began and glanced toward the coffeepot.

"Now, drink up," Julia instructed. "You need roses in your cheeks. You look terrible."

"Thanks."

Steaming chicken soup joined the milk, and Autumn attacked it with singleminded intensity. Some of the weakness drained from her limbs.

"Good girl," Julia approved as she dished up the omelette. "You look nearly human again."

Glancing over, Autumn smiled. "Julia, you're marvelous."

"Yes, I know. I was born that way." She sipped coffee and watched Autumn start on the eggs. "I'm glad you were able to rest. This day has been a century."

For the first time, Autumn noticed the mauve shadows under the blue eyes and felt a tug of guilt. "I'm sorry. You should be in bed, not waiting on me."

"Lord, but you're sweet." Julia pulled out a cigarette. "I haven't any desire to go up to my room until exhaustion takes over. I'm quite selfishly prepared to keep you with me until it does. Actually, Autumn," she added, watching through a mist of smoke, "I wonder if it's very wise for you to be wandering about on your own."

"What?" Autumn looked up again and frowned. "What do you mean?"

"It was your room that was broken into," Julia pointed out.

"Yes, but..." She was surprised to realize she'd almost overlooked the ransacking of her room with everything else that had happened. "It must have been Helen," she ventured.

"Oh, I doubt that," Julia returned and continued to sip contemplatively. "I very much doubt that. If Helen had broken into your room, it would have been to look for something she could use on you. She'd have been tidy. We've given this some thought."

"We?"

"Well, I've given it some thought," Julia amended smoothly. "I think whoever tore up your things was looking for something, then covered the search with overdone destruction."

"Looking for what?" Autumn demanded. "I don't have anything anyone here could be interested in."

"Don't you?" Julia ran the tip of her tongue over her teeth. "I've been thinking about what happened in your darkroom."

"You mean when the power went off?" Autumn shook her head and touched the bruise on her forehead. "I walked into the door."

"Did you?" Julia sat back and studied the harsh ceiling light. "I wonder. Lucas told me that you said you heard someone rattling at the knob and walked over. What if..." She brought her eyes back to Autumn's. "What if someone swung the door open and hit you with it?"

"It was locked," Autumn insisted, then remembered that it had been open when Lucas found her.

"There are keys, darling." She watched Autumn's face closely. "What are you thinking?"

"The door was open when Lucas—" She cut herself off and shook her head. "No, Julia, it's ridiculous. Why would anyone want to do that to me?"

Julia lifted a brow. "Interesting question. What about your ruined film?"

"The film?" Autumn felt herself being pulled in deeper. "It must have been an accident."

"You didn't spoil it, Autumn, you're too competent." She waited while Autumn spread her hands on the table and looked down at them. "I've watched you. Your movements are very fluid, very assured. And you're a professional. You wouldn't botch up a roll of film without being aware of it."

"No," Autumn agreed and looked back up. Her eyes were steady again. "What are you trying to tell me?"

"What if someone's worried that you took a picture they don't want developed? The film in your room was ruined, too."

"I can follow your logic that far, Julia." Autumn pushed aside the remaining omelette. "But then it's a dead end. I haven't taken any pictures anyone could worry about. I was shooting scenery. Trees, animals, the lake.''

"Maybe someone isn't certain about that." She crushed out her cigarette in a quick motion and leaned forward. "Whoever is worried enough about a picture to risk destroying your room and knocking you unconscious is dangerous. Dangerous enough to murder. Dangerous enough to hurt you again if necessary."

Staring back, Autumn controlled a tremor. "Jane? Jane accused me of spying, but she couldn't—"

"Oh yes, she could." Julia's voice was hard again, and definite. "Face it, Autumn, anyone pushed hard enough is capable of murder. Anyone."

Autumn's thoughts flicked back to Lucas and the look on his face when he had slipped his hand around her throat.

"Jane was desperate," Julia continued. "She claims to have made a full confession to Robert, but what proof is there? Or Robert, furious at what Helen had put his wife through, could have done it himself. He loves Jane quite a lot."

"Yes, I know." The sudden, sweeping anger in Robert's eyes flashed through her mind.

"Or there's Steve." Julia's finger began to tap on the table. "He tells me that Helen found out about some unwise deal he put through, something potentially damaging to his political career. He's very ambitious.''

"But, Julia—"

"Then there's Lucas." Julia went on as if Autumn hadn't spoken. "There's a matter of a delicate divorce suit. Helen held information she claimed would interest a certain estranged husband." She lit another cigarette and let the smile float up and away. "Lucas is known for his temper. He's a very physical man."

Autumn met the look steadily. "Lucas is a lot of things, not all of them admirable, but he wouldn't kill."

Julia smiled and said nothing as she brought the cigarette to her lips. "Then there's me." The smile widened. "Of course, I claim I didn't care about Helen's threats, but I'm an actress. A good one. I've got an Oscar to prove it. Like Lucas, my temper is no secret. I could give you a list of directors who would tell you I'm capable of anything." Idly she tapped her cigarette in the ashtray. "But then, if I had killed her, I would have set the scene differently. I would have discovered the body myself, screamed, then fainted magnificently. As it was, you stole the show."

"That's not funny, Julia."

"No," she agreed and rubbed her temple. "It's not. But the fact remains that I could have killed Helen, and you're far too trusting."

"If you'd killed her," Autumn countered, "why would you warn me?"

"Bluff and double bluff," Julia answered with a new smile that made Autumn's skin crawl. "Don't trust anyone, not even me."

Autumn wasn't going to let Julia frighten her, though she seemed determined to do so. She kept her eyes level. "You haven't included Jacques."

To Autumn's surprise, Julia's eyes flickered, then dropped. The smooth, tapering fingers crushed out her cigarette with enough force to break the filter. "No, I haven't. I suppose he must be viewed through your eyes like the rest of us, but I know..." She looked up again, and Autumn saw the vulnerability. "I know he isn't capable of hurting anyone."

"You're in love with him."

Julia smiled, quite beautifully. "I love Jacques very much, but not the way you mean." She rose then and, getting another cup, poured them both coffee. "I've known Jacques for ten years. He's the only person in the world I care about more than myself. We're friends, real friends, probably because we've never been lovers.''

Autumn drank the coffee black. She wanted the kick of it. *She'd protect him,* she thought. *She'd protect him any way she could.*

''I have a weakness for men,'' Julia continued, ''and I indulge it. With Jacques, the time or place was never right. Ultimately, the friendship was too important to risk messing it up in the bedroom. He's a good, gentle man. The biggest mistake he ever made was in marrying Claudette.''

Julia's voice hardened. Her nails began to tap on the table again, quicker than before. ''She did her best to eat him alive. For a long time, he tried to keep the marriage together for the children. It simply wasn't possible. I won't go into details; they'd shock you.'' Tilting her head, Julia gave Autumn a smile that put her squarely into adolescence. ''And, in any case, it's Jacques's miserable secret. He didn't divorce her, on the numerous grounds he could have, but allowed her to file.''

''And Claudette got the children.''

''That's right. It nearly killed him when she was awarded custody. He adores them. And, I must admit, they are rather sweet little monsters.'' The nails stopped tapping as she reached for her coffee. ''Anyway, skipping over this and that, Jacques filed a custody suit about a year ago. He met someone shortly after. I can't tell you her name—you'd recognize it, and I have Jacques's confidence. But I can tell you she's perfect for him. Then Helen crawled her slimy way in."

Autumn shook her head. "Why don't they just get married?"

Julia leaned back with an amused sigh. "If life were only so simple. Jacques is free, but his lady won't be for another few months. They want nothing more than to marry, bring Jacques's little monsters to America and raise as many more as possible. They're crazy about each other."

Julia sipped her cooling coffee. "They can't live together openly until the custody thing is resolved so they rented this little place in the country. Helen found out. You can figure out the rest. Jacques paid her, for his children and because his lady's divorce isn't as cut-and-dried as it might be, but when Helen turned up here, he'd reached his limit. They argued about it one night in the lounge. He told her she wouldn't get another cent. I'm sure, no matter how much Jacques had already paid her, Helen would still have turned her information over to Claudette—for a price."

Autumn stared at her, unable to speak. She had never seen Julia look so cold. She saw the ruthlessness cover the exquisite face. Julia looked over, then laughed with genuine amusement.

"Oh, Autumn, you're like an open book!" The hard mask had melted away, leaving her warm and lovely again. "Now you're thinking I could have murdered Helen after all. Not for myself, but for Jacques."

Autumn fell into a fitful sleep sometime after dawn. This was no deep, empty sleep brought on by medication or exhaustion, but was confused and dream riddled.

At first, there were only vague shadows and murmured voices floating through her mind, taunting her to try to see and hear more clearly. She fought to focus on them. Shadows moved, shapes began to sharpen, then became fuzzy and disordered again. She pitted all her determination against them, wanting more than hints and whispers. Abruptly, the shadows evaporated. The voices grew to a roar in her ears.

Wild-eyed, Jane crushed Autumn's camera underfoot. She screamed, pointing a pair of scissors to keep Autumn at bay. "Spy!" she shouted as the cracking of the camera's glass echoed like gunfire. "Spy!"

Wanting to escape the madness and accusations, Autumn turned. Colors whirled around her, then there was Robert.

"She tormented my wife." His arm held Autumn firmly, then slowly tightened, cutting off her breath. "You need some food," he said softly. "It shows in the face first." He was smiling, but the smile was a travesty. Breaking away, Autumn found herself in the corridor.

Jacques came toward her. There was blood on his hands. His eyes were sad and terrifying as he held them out to her. "My children." There was a tremor in his voice as he gestured to her. Turning, she fell into Steve.

"Politics," he said with a bright, boyish smile. "Nothing personal, just politics." Taking her hair, he wrapped it around her throat. "You got caught in the middle, Autumn." The smile turned into a leer as he tightened the noose. "Too bad."

Pushing away, she fell through a door. Julia's back was to her. She wore the lovely, white lace negligee. "Julia!" In the dream, the urgency in Autumn's voice came at a snail's pace. "Julia, help me."

When Julia turned, the slow, cat smile was on her face and the lace was splattered with scarlet. "Bluff and double bluff, darling." Throwing back her head, she laughed her smoky laugh. With the sound still spinning in her head, Autumn pressed her hands to her ears and ran.

"Come back to mother!" Julia called, still laughing as Autumn stumbled into the corridor.

There was a door blocking her path. Throwing it open, Autumn dashed inside. She knew only a desperate need for escape. But it was Helen's room. Terrified, Autumn turned, only to find the door closed behind her. She battered on it, but the sound was dull and flat. Fear was raw now, a primitive fear of the dead. She couldn't stay there. Wouldn't stay. She turned, thinking to escape through the window.

It wasn't Helen's room, but her own. There were bars at the windows, gray liquid bars of rain, but when she ran to them, they solidified, holding her in. She pulled and tugged, but they were cold and unyielding in her hands. Suddenly, Lucas was behind her, drawing her away. He laughed as he turned her into his arms.

"Bite and scratch all you want, Cat."

"Lucas, please!" There was hysteria in her voice that even the dream couldn't muffle. "I love you. I love you. Help me get out. Help me get away!''

"Too late, Cat." His eyes were dark and fierce and amused. "I warned you not to push me too far."

"No, Lucas, not you." She clung to him. He was kissing her hard, passionately. "I love you. I've always loved you." She surrendered to his arms, to his mouth. Here was her escape, her safety.

Then she saw the scissors in his hand.

Chapter Ten

Autumn sat straight up in bed. The film of cold sweat had her shivering. During the nightmare, she had kicked off the sheets and blankets and lay now with only a damp nightgown for cover. Needing the warmth, she pulled the tangled blanket around her and huddled into it.

Only a dream, she told herself, waiting for the clarity of it to fade. It was only a dream. It was natural enough after the late-night conversation with Julia. Dreams couldn't hurt you. Autumn wanted to hang on to that.

It was morning. She trembled still as she watched the sunlight pour into her window. No bars. That was over now, just as the night was over. The phones would soon be repaired. The water in the ford would go down. The police would come. Autumn sat, cocooned by the blanket, and waited for her breathing to even.

By the end of the day, or tomorrow at the latest, everything would be organized and official. Questions would be answered, notes would be taken, the wheels of investigation would start to turn, settling everything into facts and reality. Slowly her muscles began to relax and she loosened her desperate grip on the blanket.

Julia's imagination had gotten out of hand, Autumn decided. She was so used to the drama of her profession that she had built up the scenario. Helen's death was a hard, cold fact. None of them could avoid that. But Autumn was certain her two misfortunes had been unconnected. If I'm going to stay sane until the police come, she amended, I *have* to believe it.

Calmer now, she allowed herself to think. Yes, there had been a murder. There was no glossing over that. Murder was a violent act, and in this case, it had been a personal one. She had no involvement in it. There wasn't any correlation. What had happened in the darkroom had been simple clumsiness. That was the cleanest and the most reasonable explanation. As for the invasion of her room... Autumn shrugged. It had been Helen. She'd been a vicious, evil woman. The destruction of Autumn's clothes and personal belongings had been a vicious, evil act. For some reason of her own, Helen had taken a dislike to her. There was no one else at the inn who would have any reason to feel hostility toward her.

Except Lucas. Autumn shook her head firmly, but the thought remained. Except Lucas. She huddled the blanket closer, cold again.

No, even that made no sense. Lucas had rejected her, not the other way around. She had loved him. And he, very simply, hadn't loved her. *Would that matter to him?* The voice in her brain argued with the voice from her heart. Ignoring the queaziness in her stomach, Autumn forced herself to consider, dispassionately, Lucas in the role of murderer.

It had been obvious from the beginning that he was under strain. He hadn't been sleeping well and he'd been tense. Autumn had known him to struggle over a stage of a book for a week on little sleep and coffee, but he'd never shown the effects. All that stored energy he had was just waiting to take over whenever he needed it. No, in all her memory, she had never seen Lucas McLean tired. Until now.

Helen's blackmail must have disturbed him deeply. Autumn couldn't imagine Lucas concerning himself over publicity, adverse or otherwise. The woman involved in divorce must mean a great deal to him. She shut her eyes on a flash of pain and forced herself to continue.

Why had he come to the Pine View Inn? Why would he choose a remote place nearly a continent away from his home? To work? Autumn shook her head. It just didn't follow. She knew Lucas never traveled when he was writing. He'd do his research first, extensively if necessary, before he began. Once he had a plot between his teeth, he'd dig into his beachside home for the duration. Come to Virginia to write in peace? No. Lucas McLean could write on the 5:15 subway if he chose to. She knew no one else with a greater ability to block people out.

So, his reason for coming to the inn was quite different. Autumn began to wonder if Helen had been a pawn as well as a manipulator. Had Lucas lured her to this remote spot and surrounded her with people with reasons to hate her? He was clever enough to have done it, and calculating enough. How difficult was it going to be to prove which one of the six had killed her? Motive and opportunity he'd said— six people had both. Why should one be examined any closer than the others?

The setting would appeal to him, she thought as she looked out at mountains and pines. Obvious, Lucas had called it. An obvious setting for murder. But then, as Jacques had pointed out, life was often obvious.

She wouldn't dwell on it. It brought the nightmare too close again. Pushing herself from the bed, Autumn began to dress in her very tired jeans and a sweater Julia had given her the night before. She wasn't going to spend another day picking at her doubts and fears. It would be better to hang on to the knowledge that the police would be there soon. It wasn't up to her to decide who had killed Helen.

When she started down the stairs, she felt better. She'd take a long, solitary walk after breakfast and clear the cobwebs from her mind. The thought of getting out of the inn lifted her spirits.

But her confidence dropped away when she saw Lucas at the foot of the stairs. He was watching her closely, silently. Their eyes met for one brief, devastating moment before he turned to walk away.

"Lucas." She heard herself call out before she could stop herself. Stopping, he turned to face her again. Autumn gathered all her courage and hurried down the rest of the stairs. She had questions, and she had to ask them. He still mattered much too much to her. She stood on the bottom step so that their eyes would be level. His told her nothing. They seemed to look through her, bored and impatient.

"Why did you come here?" Autumn asked him quickly. "Here, to the Pine View Inn?" She wanted him to give her any reason. She wanted to accept it.

Lucas focused on her intensely for a moment. There was something in his face for her to read, but it was gone before she could decipher it. "Let's just say I came to write, Autumn. Any other reason has been eliminated."

There was no expression in his voice, but the words chilled her. *Eliminated.* Would he choose such a clean word for murder? Something of her horror showed in her face. She watched his brows draw together in a frown.

"Cat—"

"No." Before he could speak again, she darted away from him. He'd given her an answer, but it wasn't one she wanted to accept.

The others were already at the table. The sun had superficially lightened the mood, and by unspoken agreement, the conversation was general, with no mention of Helen. They all needed an island of normalcy before the police came.

Julia, looking fresh and lovely, chattered away. Her attitude was so easy, even cheerful, that Autumn wondered if their conversation in the kitchen was as insubstantial as her nightmare. She was flirting again, with every man at the table. Two days of horror hadn't dulled her style.

"Your aunt," Jacques told Autumn, "has an amazing cuisine." He speared a fluffy, light pancake. "It surprises me at times because she has such a charming, drifting way about her. Yet, she remembers small details. This morning, she tells me she has saved me a piece of her apple pie to enjoy with my lunch. She doesn't forget I have a fondness for it. Then when I kiss her hand because I find her so enchanting, she smiled and wandered away, and I heard her say something about towels and chocolate pudding."

The laughter that followed was so normal, Autumn wanted to hug it to her. "She has a better memory about the guests' appetites than her family's," Autumn countered, smiling at him. "She's decided that pot roast is my favorite and has promised to provide it weekly, but it's actually my brother Paul's favorite. I haven't figured out how to move her toward spaghetti."

She gripped her fork tightly at a sudden flash of pain. Very clearly, Autumn could see herself stirring spaghetti sauce in Lucas's kitchen while he did his best to distract her. Would she never pry herself loose from the memories? Quickly, she plunged into conversation again.

"Aunt Tabby sort of floats around the rest of the world," she continued. "I remember once, when we were kids, Paul smuggled some formaldehyde frog legs out of his biology class.

He brought them with him when we came on vacation and gave them to Aunt Tabby, hoping for a few screams. She took them, smiled and told him she'd eat them later.''

"Oh, God.'' Julia lifted her hand to her throat. "She didn't actually eat them, did she?''

"No.'' Autumn grinned. "I distracted her, which of course is the easiest thing in the world to do, and Paul disposed of his biology project. She never missed them.''

"I must remember to thank my parents for making me an only child,'' Julia murmured.

"I can't imagine growing up without Paul and Will.'' Autumn shook her head as old memories ran through her mind. "The three of us were always very close, even when we tormented each other.''

Jacques chuckled, obviously thinking of his own children. "Does your family spend much time here?''

"Not as much as we used to.'' Autumn lifted her shoulders. "When I was a girl, we'd all come for a month during the summer.''

"To tramp through the woods?'' Julia asked with a wicked gleam in her eyes.

"That,'' Autumn returned mildly, and imitated the actress's arched-brow look, "and some camping.'' She went on, amused by Julia's rolling eyes. "Boating and swimming in the lake."

"Boating," Robert spoke up, cutting off a small, nagging memory. Autumn looked over at him, unable to hang onto it. "That's my one true vice. Nothing I like better than sailing. Right, Jane?" He patted her hand. "Jane's quite a sailor herself. Best first mate I've ever had." He glanced over at Steve. "I suppose you've done your share of sailing."

Steve answered with a rueful shake of his head. "I'm afraid I'm a miserable sailor. I can't even swim."

"You're joking!" This came from Julia. She stared at him in disbelief. Her eyes skimmed approvingly over his shoulders. "You look like you could handle the English Channel."

"I can't even handle a wading pool," he confessed, more amused than embarrassed. He grinned and gestured with his fork. "I make up for it in land sports. If we had a tennis court here, I'd redeem myself."

"Ah well." Jacques gave his French shrug. "You'll have to content yourself with hiking. The mountains here are beautiful. I hope to bring my children one day." He frowned, then stared into his coffee.

"Nature lovers!" Julia's smiling taunt kept the room from sliding into gloom. "Give me

smog-filled L.A. anytime. I'll look at your
mountains and squirrels in Autumn's photographs.''

"You'll have to wait until I add to my sup-
ply." She kept her voice light, trying not to be
depressed over the loss of her film. She
couldn't yet bring herself to think of the loss of
her camera. "Losing that film is like losing a
limb, but I'm trying to be brave about it."
Taking a bite of pancake, she shrugged. "And
I could have lost all four rolls instead of three.
The shots I took of the lake were the best, so I
can comfort myself with that. The light was
perfect that morning, and the shadows..."

She trailed off as the memory seeped
through. She could see herself, standing on the
ridge looking down at the glistening water, the
mirrored trees. And the two figures that walked
the far side. That was the morning she had met
Lucas in the woods, then Helen. Helen with an
angry bruise under her eye.

"Autumn?"

Hearing Jacques's voice, she snapped herself back. "I'm sorry, what?"

"Is something wrong?"

"No, I..." She met his curious eyes. "No."

"I would think light and shadow are the very
essence of photography," Julia commented,
flowing over the awkward silence. "But I've

always concerned myself with looking into the lens rather than through. Remember that horrible little man, Jacques, who used to pop up at the most extraordinary times and stick a camera in my face. What was his name? I really became quite fond of him.''

Julia had centered the attention on herself so smoothly that Autumn doubted anyone had noticed her own confusion. She stared down at the pancakes and syrup on her plate as if the solution to the mysteries of the universe were written there. But she could feel Lucas's eyes boring into her averted head. She could feel them, but she couldn't look at him.

She wanted to be alone, to think, to reason out what was whirling in her head. She forced down the rest of her breakfast and let the conversation buzz around her.

"I have to see Aunt Tabby," Autumn murmured, at last thinking she could leave without causing curiosity. "Excuse me." She had reached the kitchen door before Julia waylaid her.

"Autumn, I want to talk to you." The grip of the slender fingers was quite firm. "Come up to my room."

From the expression on the enviable face, Autumn could see arguing was useless. "All right, right after I see Aunt Tabby. She'll be worried because I didn't say good night to her yesterday. I'll be up in a few minutes.'' She kept her voice reasonable and friendly, and managed a smile. Autumn decided she was becoming quite an actress herself.

For a small stretch of silence, Julia studied Autumn's face, then loosened her grip. ''All right, come up as soon as you've finished.''

''Yes, I will.'' Autumn slipped into the kitchen with the promise still on her lips. It wasn't difficult to go through the kitchen to the mud room without being noticed. Aunt Tabby and Nancy were deep in their morning argument. Taking down her jacket from the hook where she had placed it the morning of the storm, Autumn checked the pocket. Her fingers closed over the roll of film. For a moment, she simply held it in the palm of her hand.

Moving quickly, she changed from shoes to boots, transferred the film to the pocket of Julia's sweater, grabbed her jacket and went out the back door.

Chapter Eleven

The air was sharp. The rain had washed it clean. Budded leaves Autumn had photographed only days before were fuller, thicker, but still tenderly green. Her mind was no longer on the freedom she had longed for all the previous day. Now, Autumn was only intent on reaching the cover of the forest without being seen. She ran for the trees, not stopping until she was surrounded. Silence was deep and it cradled her.

The ground sucked and skidded under her feet, spongy with rain. There was some wind damage here and there that she noticed when she forced herself to move more carefully. Broken limbs littered the ground. The sun was warm, and she shed her jacket, tossing it over a branch. She made herself concentrate on the sights and sounds of the forest until her thoughts could calm.

The mountain laurel hinted at blooms. A bird circled overhead, then darted deeper into the trees with a sharp cry. A squirrel scurried up a tree trunk and peered down at her. Autumn reached in her pocket and closed her hand over the roll of film. The conversation in the kitchen with Julia now made horrible sense.

Helen must have been at the lake that morning. From the evidence of the bruise, she had argued violently with someone. And that someone had seen Autumn on the ridge. That someone wanted the pictures destroyed badly enough to risk breaking into both her darkroom and her bedroom. The film had to be potentially damaging for anyone to risk knocking her unconscious and ransacking her room. Who else but the killer would care enough to take such dangerous actions? Who else? At every turn, logic pointed its finger toward Lucas.

It had been his plans that brought the group together in the first place. Lucas was the person Autumn had met just before coming across Helen. Lucas had bent over her as she lay on the darkroom floor. Lucas had been up, fully dressed, the night of Helen's murder. Autumn shook her head, wanting to shatter the logic. But the film was solid in her hand.

He must have seen her as she stood on the ridge. She would have been in clear view. When he intercepted her, he had tried to rekindle their relationship. He would have known better than to have attempted to remove the film from her camera. She would have caused a commotion that would have been heard in two counties. Yes, he knew her well enough to use subtler means. But he wouldn't have known she had already switched to a fresh roll.

He had played on her old weakness for him. If she had submitted, he would have found ample time and opportunity to destroy the film. Autumn admitted, painfully, that she would have been too involved with him to have noticed the loss. But she hadn't submitted. This time, she had rejected him. He would have been forced to employ more extreme measures.

He only pretended to want me, she realized. That, more than anything else, hurt. He had held her, kissed her, while his mind had been busy calculating how best to protect himself. Autumn forced herself to face facts. Lucas had stopped wanting her a long time ago, and his needs had never been the same as hers. Two facts were very clear. She had never stopped loving him, and he had never begun to love her.

Still, she balked at the idea of Lucas as a cold-blooded killer. She could remember his sudden spurts of gentleness, his humor, the careless bouts of generosity. That was part of him, too—part of the reason she had been able to love him so easily. Part of the reason she had never stopped.

A hand gripped her shoulder. With a quick cry of alarm, she whirled and found herself face-to-face with Lucas. When she shrank from him, he dropped his hands and stuffed them into his pockets. His eyes were dark and his voice was icy.

"Where's the film, Autumn?"

Whatever color left in her face drained. She hadn't wanted to believe it. Part of her had refused to believe it. Now, her heart shattered. He was leaving her no choice.

"Film?" She shook her head as she took another step back. "What film?"

"You know very well what film." Impatience pulled at the words. He narrowed his eyes, watching her retreat. "I want the fourth roll. Don't back away from me!"

Autumn stopped at the curt command. "Why?"

"Don't play stupid." His impatience was quickly becoming fury. She recognized all the signs. "I want the film. What I do with it is my business."

She ran, thinking only to escape from his words. It had been easier to live with the doubt than the certainty. He caught her arm before she had dashed three yards. Spinning her around, he studied her face.

"You're terrified." He looked stunned, then angry. "You're terrified of me." With his hands gripping hard on her arms he brought her closer. "We've run the gamut, haven't we, Cat? Yesterday's gone." There was a finality in his voice that brought more pain than his hands or his temper.

"Lucas." Autumn was trembling, emotionally spent. "Please don't hurt me anymore." The pain she spoke of had nothing to do with the physical, but he released her with a violent jerk. The struggle for control was visible on his face.

"I won't lay a hand on you now, or ever again. Just tell me where that film is. I'll get out of your life as quickly as possible."

She had to reach him. She had to try one last time. "Lucas, please, it's senseless. You must see that. Can't you—"

"Don't push me!" The words exploded at her, rocking her back on her heels. "You stupid fool, do you have any idea how dangerous that film is? Do you think for one minute I'm going to let you keep it?" He took a step toward her. "Tell me where it is. Tell me now, or by God, I'll throttle it out of you."

"In the darkroom." The lie came quickly and without calculation. Perhaps that was why he accepted it so readily.

"All right. Where?" She watched his features relax slightly. His voice was calmer.

"On the bottom shelf. On the wet side."

"That's hardly illuminating to a layman, Cat." There was a touch of his old mockery as he reached for her arm. "Let's go get it."

"No!" She jerked away wildly. "I won't go with you. There's only one roll; you'll find it. You found the others. Leave me alone, Lucas. For God's sake, leave me alone!"

She ran again, skidding on the mud. This time he didn't stop her.

Autumn had no idea how far she ran or even the direction she took. Ultimately, her feet slowed to a walk. She stopped to stare up at a sky that had no clouds. What was she going to do?

She could go back. She could go back and try to get to the darkroom first, lock herself in. She could develop the film, blow up the two figures beside the lake and see the truth for herself. Her hand reached for the hated film again. She didn't want to see the truth. With absolute certainty, she knew she could never hand the film over to the police. No matter what Lucas had done or would do, she couldn't betray him. He'd been wrong, she thought. She could never pull the lever.

Withdrawing the film from her pocket, she stared down at it. It looked so innocent. She had felt so innocent that day, up on the ridge with the sun coming up. But when she had done what she had to do, she would never feel innocent again. She would expose the film herself.

Lucas, she thought and nearly laughed. Lucas McLean was the only man on earth who could make her turn her back on her own conscience. And when it was done, only the two of them would know. She would be as guilty as he.

Do it quickly, she told herself. Do it fast and think about it later. Her palm was damp where the film was cradled in it. You're going to have a whole lifetime to think about it. Taking a deep breath, Autumn started to uncap the plastic capsule she used to protect her undeveloped film. A movement on the path behind her had her stuffing the roll back into her pocket and whirling around.

Could Lucas have searched the darkroom so quickly? What would he do now that he knew she had lied to him? Foolishly, Autumn wanted to run again. Instead, she straightened and waited. The final encounter would have to come sooner or later.

Autumn's relief when she saw Steve approaching quickly became irritation. She wanted to be alone, not to make small talk and useless conversation while the film burned in her pocket.

"Hi!" Steve's lightning smile did nothing to decrease her annoyance, but Autumn pasted on one of her own. If she were going to be playing a game for the rest of her life, she might as well start now.

"Hello. Taking Jacques up on the hiking?" God, how normal and shallow her voice sounded! Was she going to be able to live like this?

"Yeah. I see you needed to get away from the inn, too." Taking a deep breath of the freshened air, he flexed his shoulders. "Lord, it feels good to be outside again."

"I know what you mean." Autumn eased the tension from her own shoulders. This was a reprieve, she told herself. Accept it. When it's over, nothing's ever going to be the same again.

"And Jacques is right," Steve went on, staring out through the thin leaves. "The mountains are beautiful. It reminds you that life goes on."

"I suppose we all need to remember that now." Unconsciously, Autumn dipped her hand in her pocket.

"Your hair glows in the sunlight." Steve caught at the ends and moved them between his fingertips. Autumn saw, with some alarm, that warmth had crept into his eyes. A romantic interlude was more than she could handle.

"People often seem to think more about my hair than me." She smiled and kept her voice light. "Sometimes I'm tempted to hack it off."

"Oh no." He took a more generous handful. "It's very special, very unique." His eyes lifted to hers. "And I've been thinking quite a lot about you the last few days. You're very special, too."

"Steve..." Autumn turned and would have walked on, but his hand was still in her hair.

"I want you, Autumn."

The words, so gentle, almost humble, nearly broke her heart. She turned back with apology in her eyes. "I'm sorry, Steve. I really am."

"Don't be sorry." He lowered his head to brush her lips. "If you let me, I could make you happy."

"Steve, please." Autumn lifted her hands to his chest. If only he were Lucas, she thought as she stared up at him. If only it were Lucas looking at me like this. "I can't."

He let out a long breath, but didn't release her. "McLean? Autumn, he only makes you unhappy. Why won't you let go?"

"I can't tell you how many times I've asked myself the same question." She sighed, and he watched the sun shoot into her eyes. "I don't have the answer—except that I love him."

"Yes, it shows." Frowning, he brushed a strand of hair from her cheek. "I'd hoped you'd be able to get over him, but I don't suppose you will."

"No, I don't suppose I will. I've given up trying."

"Now I'm sorry, Autumn. It makes things difficult."

Autumn dropped her eyes to stare at the ground. She didn't want pity. "Steve, I appreciate it, but I really need to be alone."

"I want the film, Autumn."

Astonished, she jerked her head up. Without consciously making the step, she aligned herself with Lucas. "Film? I don't know what you mean."

"Oh yes, I'm afraid you do." He was still speaking gently, one hand stroking her hair. "The pictures you took of the lake the morning Helen and I were down there. I have to have them."

"You?" For a moment, the implication eluded her. "You and Helen?" Confusion turned into shock. She could only stare at him.

"We were having quite a row that morning. You see, she had decided she wanted a lump-sum payment from me. Her other sources were drying up fast. Julia wouldn't give her a penny, just laughed at her. Helen was furious about that." His face changed with a grim smile. "Jacques had finished with her, too. She never had anything worthwhile on Lucas in the first place. She counted on intimidating him. Instead, he told her to go to hell and threatened to press charges. That threw her off balance for a while. She must have realized Jane was on the edge. So...she concentrated on me."

He had been staring off into the distance as he spoke. Now, his attention came back to Autumn. The first hint of anger swept into his eyes. "She wanted two hundred and fifty thousand dollars in two weeks. A quarter of a million, or she'd hand over the information she had on me to my father."

"But you said what she knew wasn't important." Autumn let her eyes dart past his for a moment. The path behind them was empty. She was alone.

"She knew a bit more than I told you." Steve gave her an apologetic smile. "I could hardly tell you everything then. I've covered my tracks well enough now so that I don't think the police will ever know. It was actually a matter of extortion.''

"Extortion?'' The hand on her hair was becoming more terrifying with each passing moment. Keep him talking, she told herself frantically. Keep him talking and someone will come.

"Borrowing, really. The money will be mine sooner or later.'' He shrugged it off. "I just took some a little early. Unfortunately, my father wouldn't see it that way. I told you, remember? He's a tough man. He wouldn't think twice about booting me out the door and cutting off my income. I can't have that, Autumn.'' He flashed her a smile. "I have very expensive tastes.''

"So you killed her.'' Autumn said it flatly. She was finished with horror.

"I didn't have a choice. I couldn't possibly get my hands on that much cash in two weeks.'' He said it so calmly, Autumn could almost see the rationale behind it. "I nearly killed her that morning down by the lake. She just wouldn't listen to me. I lost my temper and hit her. Knocked her cold. When I saw her lying there on the ground, I realized how much I wanted her dead.''

Autumn didn't interrupt. She could see he was far from finished. Let him talk it out, she ordered herself, controlling the urge to break from him and run. Someone's going to come.

"I bent over her," he continued. "My hands were almost around her throat when I saw you standing up on the ridge. I knew it was you because the sun was shining on your hair. I didn't think you could recognize me from that distance, but I had to be sure. Of course, I found out later that you weren't paying attention to us at all."

"No, I barely noticed." Her knees were starting to shake. He was telling her too much. Far too much.

"I left Helen and circled around, thinking to intercept you. Lucas got to you first. Quite a touching little scene."

"You watched us?" She felt a stir of anger edge through the fear.

"You were too involved in each other to notice." He smiled again. "In any case, that's when I learned you'd been taking pictures. I had to get rid of that film; it was too chancy. I hated to hurt you, Autumn. I found you very attractive right from the first."

A rabbit darted down the path, veering off and bounding into the woods. She heard the call of a quail, faint with distance. The simple, natural texture of her surroundings gave his words a sense of unreality. "The darkroom."

"Yes. I was glad the blow with the door knocked you out. I didn't want to have to hit you with the flashlight. I didn't see your camera, but found a roll of film. I was so certain I had things taken care of. You can imagine how I felt when you said you'd lost two rolls, and that they were shots of your trip down from New York. I didn't know how the other roll had been ruined."

"Lucas. Lucas turned on the lights when he found me." Suddenly, through the horror came a bright flash of realization. *It hadn't been Lucas.* He'd done nothing but simply be who he was. She felt overwhelming relief at his innocence, then guilt at ever having believed what she had of him. "Lucas," she said again, almost giddy with the onslaught of sensations.

"Well, it hardly matters now," Steve said practically. Autumn snapped back. She had to keep alert, had to keep a step ahead of him. "I knew if I just took the film from your camera, you'd begin to wonder. You might start thinking too closely about the pictures you'd taken. I hated doing that to your things, breaking your camera. I know it was important to you."

"I have another at home." It was a weak attempt to sound unconcerned. Steve only smiled.

"I went to Helen's room right after I'd finished with yours. I knew I was going to have to kill her. She stood there pointing to the bruise and telling me it was going to cost me another hundred thousand. I didn't know what I was going to do... I thought I was going to strangle her. Then I saw the scissors. That was better—anyone could have used scissors. Even little Jane. I stopped thinking when I picked them up until it was over."

He shuddered, and Autumn thought, *Run! Run now!* But his hand tightened on her hair. "I've never been through anything like that. It was terrible. I almost folded. I knew I had to think, had to be careful, or I'd lose everything. Staying in that room was the hardest thing I've ever done. I wiped the handles of the scissors clean and tore up my shirt. Her blood was on it. I flushed the pieces down the toilet. When I got back to my room, I showered and went to bed. I remember being surprised that the whole thing took less than twenty minutes. It seemed like years."

"It must have been dreadful for you," Autumn murmured, but he was oblivious to the edge in her voice.

"Yes, but it was all working out. No one could prove where they were when Helen was killed. The storm—the phones, the power—that was all a bonus. Every one of us had a reason to want Helen out of the way. I really think Julia and I will be the least likely suspects when the time comes. The police should look to Jacques because he had more cause, and Lucas because he has the temper."

"Lucas couldn't kill anyone," Autumn said evenly. "The police will know that."

"I wouldn't bank on it." He gave her a crooked smile. "You haven't been so sure of that yourself."

She could say nothing when struck with the truth. *Why wasn't someone coming?*

"This morning, you started talking about four rolls of film, and the pictures you took of the lake. I could tell the moment when you remembered."

So much for my talent at acting, she thought grimly. "I only remembered there'd been people down by the lake that morning."

"You were putting it all together quickly." He traced a finger down her cheek and Autumn forced herself not to jerk away. "I had hoped to distract you, gain your affection. It was obvious you were hurting over McLean. If I could have moved in, I might have gotten my hands on that film without having to hurt you."

Autumn kept her eyes and voice steady. He'd finished talking now; she could sense it. "What are you going to do?"

"Damn it, Autumn. I'm going to have to kill you."

He said it in much the same way her father had said, *"Damn it, Autumn, I'm going to have to spank you."* She nearly broke into hysterical giggles.

"They'll know this time, Steve." Her body was beginning to shake, but she spoke calmly. If she could reason with him . . .

"No, I don't think so." He spoke practically, as if he considered she might have a viable point. "I was careful to get out without being seen. Everyone's spread out again. I doubt anyone even knows you went outside. I wouldn't have known myself if I hadn't found your jacket and boots missing. Then again, if I hadn't found the jacket hanging on a branch and been able to follow your tracks from there, I wouldn't have found you so easily."

He shrugged, as if showing her why his reasoning was better than hers. "When you're found missing, I'll make certain I come this way when we look for you. I can do a lot of damage to the tracks and no one will know any better. Now, Autumn, I need the film. Tell me where you've put it.''

"I'm not going to tell you." She tossed back her head. As long as she had the film, he had to keep her alive. "They'll find it. When they do, they'll know it was you."

He made a quick sound of impatience. "You'll tell me Autumn, eventually. It would be easier for you if you told me now. I don't want to hurt you any more than I have to. I can make it quick, or I can make it painful."

His hand shot out so swiftly, Autumn had no time to dodge the blow. The force of it knocked her back into a tree. The pain welled inside her head and rolled through, leaving dizziness. She clutched at the rough bark to keep her balance as she saw him coming toward her.

Oh no, she wasn't going to stand and be hit again. He'd gotten away with it twice, and twice was enough. With as much force as she could muster, she kicked, aiming well below the waist. He went down on his knees like a shot. Autumn turned and fled.

Chapter Twelve

She ran blindly. *Escape!* It was the only coherent thought in her brain. It wasn't until the first wave of panic had ebbed that Autumn realized she had run not only away from Steve, but away from the inn. It was too late to double back. She could only concentrate as much effort as possible into putting distance between them. She veered off the path and into thicker undergrowth.

When she heard him coming after her, Autumn didn't look back, but increased her pace. His breathing was labored, but close. Too close. She swerved again and plunged on. The ground sucked and pulled at her boots, but she told herself she wouldn't slip. If she slipped, he would be on top of her in a moment. His hands would be at her throat. *She would not slip.*

Her heart was pounding and her lungs were screaming in agony for more air. A branch whipped back, stinging her cheek. But she told herself she wouldn't stop. She would run and run and run until she no longer heard him coming after her.

A tree had fallen and lay drunkenly in her path. Without breaking stride, Autumn vaulted it, sliding for a moment when her boots hit the mud, then pounding on. He slipped. She heard the slick sound of his boots as they lost traction, then his muffled curse. She kept up her wild pace, nearly giddy at the few seconds his fall had given her.

Time and direction ceased to exist. For her, the pursuit had no beginning, no end. It was only the race. Her thoughts were no longer rational. She knew only that she had to keep running though she'd almost forgotten why. Her breath was coming in harsh gasps, her legs were like rubber. She knew only the mindless flight of the hunted—the naked fear of the hunter.

Suddenly, she saw the lake. It glistened as the sun hit its surface. With some last vestige of lucidity, Autumn remembered Steve's admission that morning. He couldn't swim. The race had a goal now, and she dashed for it.

Her crazed approach through the woods had taken her away from the ridge where the incline graduated for easy descent. Instead, she came to the edge of a cliff that fell forty feet in a sheer drop. Without hesitation, Autumn plunged down at full speed. She scrambled and slid, her fingers clawing to keep herself from overbalancing. Like a lizard, she clung to the mountain. Her body scraped on jagged rocks and slid on mud. Julia's designer sweater shredded. Autumn realized, as the pain grew hot, that her skin suffered equally. Fear pushed her beyond the pain. The lake beckoned below. Safety. Victory.

Still, he came after her. She could hear his boots clatter on the rocks above her head, jarring pebbles that rained down on her. Autumn leaped the last ten feet. The force of the fall shot up her legs, folding them under her until she rolled into a heap. Then she was scrambling and streaking for the lake.

She heard him cry out for her. With a final mad impetus, she flung herself into the water, slicing through its surface. Its sharp frigidity shocked her system and gave her strength. Clawing through it, she headed for depth. She was going to win.

Like a light switched off, the momentum which had driven her so wildly, sapped. The weight of her boots pulled her down. The water closed over her head. Thrashing and choking, Autumn fought for the surface. Her lungs burned as she tried to pull in air. Her arms were heavy, and her feeble strokes had her bobbing up and down. Mists gathered in front of her eyes. Still, she resisted, fighting as the water sucked at her. It was now as deadly an enemy as the one she had sought to escape.

She heard someone sobbing, and realized dimly it was her own voice calling for help. But she knew there would be none. The fight was gone out of her. Was it music she heard? She thought it came from below her, deep, beckoning. Slowly, surrendering, she let the water take her like a lover.

Someone was hurting her. Autumn didn't protest. Darkness blanketed her mind and numbed the pain. The pushing and prodding were no more irritating to her than a faint itch. Air forced its way into her lungs, and she moaned gently in annoyance.

Lucas's voice touched the edges of her mind. He was calling her back in a strange, unnatural voice. Panic? Yes, even through the darkness she could detect a note of panic. What an odd thing to hear in Lucas's voice. Her eyelids were heavy, and the darkness was so tempting. The need to tell him was stronger. Autumn forced her eyes open. Blackness receded to a verge of mist.

His face loomed over her, water streaming from it and his hair. It splattered cold on her cheeks. Yet her mouth felt warm, as if his had just left it. Autumn stared at him, groping for the power of speech.

"Oh God, Autumn." Lucas brushed the water from her cheeks even as it fell on them again from his own hair. "Oh God. Listen to me. It's all right, you're going to be all right, do you hear? You're going to be all right. I'm going to take you back to the inn. Can you understand me?"

His voice was desperate, as were his eyes. She'd never heard that tone or seen that expression. Not from Lucas. Autumn wanted to say something that would comfort him, but lacked the strength. The mists were closing in again, and she welcomed them. For a moment, she held them off and dug deep for her voice.

"I thought you killed her, Lucas. I'm sorry."

"Oh, Cat." His voice was intolerably weary. She felt his mouth touch hers. Then she felt nothing.

Voices, vague and without texture, floated down a long tunnel. Autumn didn't welcome them. She wanted her peace. She tried to plunge deeper into the darkness again, but Lucas had no respect for what anyone else wanted. His voice broke into her solitude, suddenly clear and, as always, demanding.

"I'm staying with her until she wakes up. I'm not leaving her."

"Lucas, you're dead on your feet." Robert's voice was low and soothing, in direct contrast to Lucas's. "I'll stay with Autumn. It's part of my job. She's probably going to be floating in and out all night. You wouldn't know what to do for her."

"Then you'll tell me what to do. I'm staying with her."

"Of course you are, dear." Aunt Tabby's voice surprised Autumn even in the dim, drifting darkness. It was so firm and strong. "Lucas will stay, Dr. Spicer. You've already said it's mainly a matter of rest, and waiting until she wakes naturally. Lucas can take care of her."

"I'll sit with you, Lucas, if you'd like... all right, but you've only to call me." Julia's voice rolled over Autumn, as smoky as the mists.

Suddenly, she wanted to ask them what was happening. What they were doing in her own private world. She struggled for words and formed a moan. A cool hand fell on her brow.

"Is she in pain?" Was that Lucas's voice? Autumn thought. Trembling? "Damn it, give her something for the pain!"

The darkness was whirling again, jumbling the sounds. Autumn let it swallow her.

She dreamed. The deep black curtain took on a velvet, moonlight texture. Lucas stared down at her. His face seemed oddly vivid for a dream. His hand felt real and cool on her cheek. "Cat, can you hear me?"

Autumn stared at him, then drew together all her scraps and rags of concentration. "Yes." She closed her eyes and let the darkness swirl.

When her eyes reopened, he was still there. Autumn swallowed. Her throat was burning dry. "Am I dead?"

"No. No, Cat, you're not dead." Lucas poured something cool down her throat. Her eyes drooped again as she tried to patch together her memory. It was too hard, and she let it go.

Pain shot through her. Unexpected and sharp, it rocketed down her arms and legs. Autumn heard someone moan pitifully. Lucas loomed over her again, his face pale in a shaft of moonlight. "It hurts," she complained.

"I know." He sat beside her and brought a cup to her lips. "Try to drink."

Floating, like a bright red balloon, Autumn felt herself drift through space. The pain had eased as she stumbled back into consciousness. "Julia's sweater," she murmured as she opened her eyes again. "It's torn. I think I tore it. I'll have to buy her another."

"Don't worry about it, Cat. Rest." Lucas's hand was on her hair and she turned her face to it, seeking reassurance. She floated again.

"I'm sure it was valuable," she murmured, nearly an hour later. "But I don't really need that new tripod. Julia lent me that sweater. I should have been more careful."

"Julia has dozens of sweaters, Cat. Don't worry."

Autumn closed her eyes, comforted. But she knew her tripod would have to wait.

"Lucas." She pulled herself back, but now the moonlight was the gray light of dawn.

"Yes, I'm here."

"Why?"

"Why what, Cat?"

"Why are you here?"

But he moved out of focus again. She never heard his answer.

Chapter Thirteen

The sunlight was strong. Used to darkness, Autumn blinked in protest.

"Ah, are you with us to stay this time, Autumn, or is this another quick visit?" Julia bent over her and patted her cheek. "There's a bit of color coming back, and you're cool. How do you feel?"

Autumn lay still for a moment and tried to find out. "Hollow," she decided, and Julia laughed.

"Trust you to think of your stomach."

"Hollow all over," Autumn countered. "Especially my head." She glanced confusedly around the room. "Have I been sick?"

"You gave us quite a scare." Julia eased down on the bed and studied her. "Don't you remember?"

"I was . . . dreaming?" Autumn's search for her memory found only bits and pieces. "Lucas was here. I was talking to him."

"Yes, he said you were drifting in and out through the night. Managed to say a word or two now and again. Did you really think I'd let you sacrifice your new tripod?'' She kissed Autumn's cheek, then held her a moment. ''God, when Lucas carried you in, we thought...'' Shaking her head briskly, she sat up. Autumn saw that her eyes were damp.

''Julia.'' Autumn squeezed her eyes a moment, but nothing came clear. ''I was supposed to come to your room, but I didn't.''

''No, you didn't. I should have dragged you with me then and there. None of this would have happened.'' She stood up again. ''It appears Lucas and I were both taken in by those big green eyes. I don't know how much time we wasted searching for that damn film before he went back to find you.''

''I don't understand. Why...'' As she reached up to brush at her hair, Autumn noticed the bandages on her hands. ''What are these for? Did I hurt myself?''

''It's all right now.'' Julia brushed away the question. ''I'd better let Lucas explain. He'll be furious that I chased him downstairs for some coffee, and you woke up.''

'Julia—''

''No more questions now.'' She cut Autumn off as she plucked a robe from a chair. ''Why don't you slip this on. You'll feel better.'' She eased the silk over Autumn's arms and covered more bandages. The sight of them brought added confusion, more juggled memories. "Just lie still and relax," Julia ordered. "Aunt Tabby already has some soup simmering, just waiting for you. I'll tell her to pour it into an enormous bowl."

She kissed Autumn again, then glided to the door. "Listen, Autumn." Julia turned back with a slow, cat smile. "He's been through hell these past twenty-four hours, but don't make it too easy for him."

Autumn frowned at the door when Julia had gone and wondered what the devil she was talking about.

Deciding she wouldn't find any answers lying in bed, Autumn dragged herself out. Every joint, every muscle revolted. She nearly succumbed to the desire to crawl back in, but curiosity was stronger. Her legs wobbled as she went to the mirror.

"Good God!" She looked, Autumn decided, even worse than she felt. The bruise on her temple had company. There was a light discoloration along her cheekbone and a few odd scratches. There was a sudden, clear memory of rough bark scraping against her hands. Lifting them, Autumn stared at the bandages. "What have I done to myself?" she asked aloud, then belted the robe to disguise the worst of the damage.

The door opened, and in the reflection she watched Lucas enter the room. He looked as though he hadn't slept in days. The lines of strain were deeper now and his chin was shadowed and unshaven. Only his eyes were the same. Dark and intense.

"You look like hell," she told him without turning. "You need some sleep."

He laughed. In a gesture of weariness she had never seen in him, he lifed his hands to run them down his face. "I might have expected it," he murmured. He sighed, then gave her a smile from the past. "You shouldn't be out of bed, Cat. You're liable to topple over any minute."

"I'm all right. At least I was before I looked in the mirror." Turning, she faced him directly. "I nearly fainted from shock."

"You are," he began in quiet, serious tones, "the most beautiful thing I've ever seen."

"Kindness to the invalid," she said, looking away. That had hurt, and she wasn't certain she could deal with any more pain. "I could use some explanations. My mind's a little fuddled."

"Robert said that was to be expected after..." He trailed off and jammed clenched fists into his pockets. "After everything that's happened."

Autumn looked again at her bandaged hands. "What did happen? I can't quite remember. I was running..." She lifted her eyes to his and searched. "In the woods, down the cliff. I..." She shook her head. There were only bits and pieces. "I tore Julia's sweater."

"God! You would latch onto a damn sweater!" His explosion had Autumn's eyes widening. "You almost drowned, and all you think about is Julia's sweater."

Her mouth trembled open. "The lake." Memory flooded back in a tidal wave. She leaned back against the dresser. "Steve. It was Steve. He killed Helen. He was chasing me. The film, I wouldn't give it to him." She swallowed, trying to keep calm. "I lied to you. I had it in my pocket. I kept running, but he was right behind me."

"Cat." She backed away, but he wrapped his arms around her. "Don't. Don't think about it. Damn it, I shouldn't have told you that way." He pressed his cheek against her hair. "I can't seem to do anything properly with you."

"No. No, let me think it through." Autumn pushed away. She wanted the details. Once she had them all, the fear would ease. "He found me in the woods after you'd gone in. He'd been with Helen down by the lake the morning I was taking pictures. He told me he had killed her. He told me everything.''

''We know all of it,'' Lucas cut her off sharply. ''He let out with everything once we got him back here. We got through to the police this morning.'' He whipped out a cigarette and lit it swiftly. ''He's already in custody. They've got your film, too, for whatever it's worth. Jacques found it on the path.''

''It must have fallen out of my pocket. Lucas, it was so strange.'' Her brow knitted as she remembered the timeless incident with Steve. ''He apologized for having to kill me. Then when I told him I wouldn't give him the film, he slugged me so hard I saw stars.''

Face thunderous, Lucas spun around and stalked to the window. He stared out without speaking.

''When he came at me again, I kicked him, hard, where I knew it would do the most damage.''

She heard Lucas mutter something so uncharacteristically vulgar she thought she misunderstood. For a time she rambled about her flight through the woods, talking more to herself than to him.

''I saw you when you started your suicidal plunge down the cliff.'' His back was still to her, his voice still rough. "How in God's name you managed to get to the bottom without cracking your skull..." Lucas turned when Autumn remained silent. "I'd been tracking you through the woods. When I saw you were making for the lake, I veered off and started for the ridge. I hoped to cut Anderson off." He pulled on his cigarette, then took a long, shuddering breath. "I saw you flying down those rocks. You never should have made it down alive. I called you, but you just kept tearing for the lake. I was on him before you hit the water."

"I heard someone call. I thought it was Steve." She pushed a bandaged hand against her temple. "All I could think about was getting into the water before he caught me. I remembered he couldn't swim. Then when I had trouble keeping myself up, I panicked and forgot all those nifty rules you learn in lifeguard class."

Very slowly, very deliberately, Lucas crushed out his cigarette. "By the time I finished kicking his head in, you were already floundering. How you got out so far after the run you'd had, and with boots that must weigh twenty pounds, I'll never know. I was a good ten yards from you when you went under the last time. You sank like a stone."

He turned away again to stare out the window. "I thought . . ." He shook his head a moment, then continued. "I thought you were dead when I dragged you out. You were dead white and you weren't breathing. At least not enough that I could tell." He took out another cigarette and this time had to fight with his lighter to get flame. He cursed and drew deeply.

"I remember you dripping on me," Autumn murmured into the silence. "Then I thought I died."

"You damn near did." The smoke came out of his lungs in a violent stream. "I must have pumped two gallons of water out of you. You came around just long enough to apologize for thinking I killed Helen."

"I'm sorry, Lucas."

"Don't!" His tone was curt as he swung around again.

"But I should never have—"

"No?" He cut her off with one angry word. "Why? It's easy enough to see how you reached your conclusions, culminating with my last attack about the film."

After a moment, Autumn trusted herself to speak. "There were so many things you said that made me think . . . and you were so angry.

When you asked me for the film, I wanted you to tell me anything.''

''But instead of explanations, I bullied you. Typical of me, though, isn't it?'' He drew a breath, but his body remained tense. ''That's another apology I owe you. I seem to have chalked up quite a few. Would you like them in a group, Cat, or one at a time?''

Autumn turned away from that. I wasn't an apology she wanted, but an explanation. ''Why did you want it, Lucas? How did you know?''

''It might be difficult for you to believe at this point, but I'm not completely inhuman. I wanted the film because I hoped, if I had it and made it known that I did, that you'd be safe. And . . .'' She turned back as a shadow crossed his face. ''I thought you knew, or had remembered what was on the film, and that you were protecting Anderson.''

''Protecting him?'' Astonishment reflected in her voice. ''Why would I do that?''

He moved his shoulders in a shrug. ''You seemed fond of him.''

''I thought he was nice,'' Autumn said slowly. ''I imagine we all did. But I hardly knew him. As it turns out, I didn't know him at all.''

''I misinterpreted your natural friendliness for something else. Then compounded the mistake by overreacting. I was furious that you gave him what you wouldn't give me. Trust, companionship. Affection.''

"Dog in the manger, Lucas?'' The words shot out icily.

A muscle twitched at the corner of his mouth in contrast to another negligent shrug. "If you like.''

"I'm sorry.'' With a sigh, Autumn pushed wearily at her hair. That was uncalled for.''

"Was it?'' he countered and crushed out his cigarette. "I doubt that. You're entitled to launch a few shafts, Cat. You've taken enough of them from me.''

"We're getting off the point.'' She moved away. Julia's silk robe whispered around her. "You thought I was protecting Steve. I'll accept that. But how did you know he needed protecting?''

"Julia and I had already pieced together a number of things. We were almost certain he was the one who had killed Helen.''

"You and Julia.'' Now she turned to him, curious. Autumn gestured with her hands, then stopped as the pain throbbed in them. "You're going to have to clear things up, Lucas. I might still be a little dim.''

"Julia and I had discussed Helen's blackmail thoroughly. Until her murder, we centered on Jacques's problem. Neither Julia nor I were concerned with the petty threats Helen held over us. After she was killed and your room broken into, we tossed around the idea that they were connected. Autumn, why don't you get back in bed. You're so pale.''

''No.'' She shook her head, warding off the creeping warmth the concern in his voice brought her. ''I'm fine. Please, don't stop now.''

He seemed about to argue, then changed his mind. ''I'd never believed you'd ruin your own film, or knock youself senseless. So, Julia and I began a process of elimination. I hadn't killed Helen, and I knew that Julia hadn't. I'd been in her room that night receiving a heated lecture on my technique with women until I came down to see you. And I'd passed Helen in the hall right before I'd gone into Julia's room, so even if Julia'd had the inclination to kill Helen, it's doubtful that she would have had two identical white negligees. There'd have been blood.'' He shrugged again. ''In any case, if Julia had killed her, she probably would have admitted it.''

''Yes.'' Autumn gave a murmured agreement and wondered what Julia's lace-clad lecture had included.

"I've known Jacques for years," Lucas continued. "He's simply not capable of killing. Julia and I all but eliminated the Spicers. Robert is entirely too dedicated to life to take one, and Jane would dissolve into tears."

Lucas began to pace. "Anderson fit the bill. And, for reasons of my own, I wanted it to be him. Our intrepid Julia copped the spare key from Aunt Tabby and searched his room for the shirt he had worn the night of the murder. I nearly strangled her when she told me she'd done it. She's quite a woman."

"Yes." Jealousy warred with affection. Affection won. "She's wonderful."

"The shirt wasn't there. Julia claims to have an unerring eye for wardrobe, and I wanted to believe her. We decided you should be put on guard without going into specifics. I thought it best if you were wary of everyone. We decided that Julia would talk to you because you'd trust her more quickly than you'd trust me. I hadn't done anything to warrant your trust."

"She frightened me pretty successfully," Autumn recalled. "I had nightmares."

"I'm sorry. It seemed the best way at the time. We thought the film had been destroyed, but we didn't want to take any chances."

"She was telling Jacques that night, wasn't she?"

"Yeah." Lucas noted the faint annoyance in her tone. "That way there would have been three of us to look out for you."

"I might have looked out for myself if I'd been told."

"No, I don't think so. Your face is a dead giveaway. That morning at breakfast when you started rambling about a fourth roll and re-membered, everything showed in your eyes."

"If I'd been prepared—"

"If you hadn't been a damn fool and had gone with Julia, we could have kept you safe."

"I wanted to think," she began, angry at being kept in the dark.

"It was my fault." Lucas held up a hand to stop her. "The whole thing's been my doing. I should have handled things differently. You'd never have been hurt if I had."

"No, Lucas." Guilt swamped her when she remembered the look on his face after he had dragged her from the lake. "I'd be dead if it weren't for you."

"Good God, Cat, don't look at me like that. I can't cope with it." He turned away. "I'm doing my best to keep my word. I'll get Robert; he'll want to examine you."

"Lucas." She wasn't going to let him walk out that door until he told her everything. "Why did you come here? And don't tell me you came to Virginia to write. I know—I remember your habits.''

Lucas turned, but kept his hand on the knob. ''I told you before, the other reason no longer exists. Leave it.''

He had retreated behind the cool, detached manner he used so well, but Autumn wasn't going to be shoved aside. ''This is my aunt's inn, Lucas. Your coming here, however indirectly, started this chain of events. I have a right to know why you came.''

For several seconds, he stared at her, then his hands sought his pockets again. ''All right,'' he agreed. ''I don't suppose I have any right to pride after this, and you deserve to get in a few licks after the way I've treated you.'' He came no closer, but his eyes locked hard on hers. ''I came here because of you. Because I had to get you back or go crazy.''

''Me?'' The pain was so sharp, Autumn laughed. She would not cry again. ''Oh Lucas, please, do better.'' She saw him flinch before he walked again to the window. ''You tossed me out, remember? You didn't want me then. You don't want me now.''

''Didn't want you!'' He whirled, knocking over a vase and sending it crashing. The anger surrounding him was fierce and vivid. ''You can't even comprehend how much I wanted

you, have wanted you all these years. I thought I'd lose my mind from wanting you."

"No, I won't listen to this." Autumn turned away to lean against the bedpost. "I won't listen."

"You asked for it. Now you'll listen."

"You told me you didn't want me," she flung at him. "I never meant anything to you. You told me it was finished and shrugged your shoulders like it had been nothing all along. Nothing, *nothing's* ever hurt me like the way you brushed me aside."

"I know what I did." The anger was gone from his voice to be replaced by strain. "I know the things I said to you while you stood there staring at me. I hated myself. I wanted you to scream, to rage, to make it easy for me to push you out. But you just stood there with tears falling down your face. I've never forgotten how you looked."

Autumn pulled herself together and faced him again. "You said you didn't want me. Why would you have said it if it weren't true?"

"Because you terrified me."

He said it so simply, she slumped down on the bed to stare at him. "Terrified you? *I* terrified *you?*"

"You don't know what you did to me—all that sweetness, all that generosity. You never asked anything of me, and yet you asked everything." He began to pace again. Autumn watched him in bewilderment. "You were an obsession, that's what I told myself. If I sent you away, hurt you badly enough to make you go, I'd be cured. The more I had of you, the more I needed. I'd wake up in the middle of the night and curse you for not being there. Then I'd curse myself for needing you there. I had to get away from you. I couldn't admit, not even to myself, that I loved you."

"Loved me?" Autumn repeated the words dumbly. "You loved me?"

"Loved then, love now and for the rest of my life." Lucas drew in a deep breath as if the words had left him shaken. "I wasn't able to tell you. I wasn't able to believe it." He stopped pacing and looked at her. "I've kept close tabs on you these past three years. I found all sorts of excuses to do so. When I found out about the inn, and your connection with it, I began to fly out here off and on. Finally, I admitted to myself that I wasn't going to make it without you. I mapped out a plan. I had it all worked out." He gave her an ironic smile.

"Plan?" Autumn repeated. Her mind was still whirling.

"It was easy to plant the idea in Aunt Tabby's head to write you and ask you to visit.

Knowing you, I was sure you'd come without question. That was all I needed. I was so sure of myself. I thought all I'd have to do would be to issue the invitation, and you'd fall right back into my arms. Just like old times. I'd have you back, marry you before you sorted things out and pat myself on the back for being so damn clever.''

"Marry me?" Autumn's brows flew up in astonishment.

"Once we were married," Lucas went on as if she hadn't interrupted, "I'd never have to worry about losing you again. I'd simply never give you a divorce no matter how you struggled. I deserved a good kick in the teeth, Cat, and you gave it to me. Instead of falling into my arms, you turned up your nose and told me to get lost. But that didn't throw me off for long. No, you'd loved me once, and I'd make you love me again. I could deal with the anger, but the ice...

"I didn't know I could be hurt that way. It was quite a shock. Seeing you again..." He paused and seemed to struggle for words. "It was torture, pure and simple, to be so close and not be able to have you. I wanted to tell you what you meant to me, then every time I got near you I'd behave like a maniac. The way you cringed from me yesterday, telling me not to hurt you again, I can't tell you what that did to me."

"Lucas—"

"You'd better let me finish," he told her. "I'll never be able to manage this again." He reached for a cigarette, changed his mind, then continued. "Julia roasted me, but I couldn't seem to stop myself. The more you resisted, the worse I treated you. Every time I approached you, I ended up doing the wrong thing. That day, up in your room..." He stopped and Autumn watched the struggle on his face. "I nearly raped you. I was crazy with jealousy after seeing you and Anderson. When I saw you cry—I swore I'd never be responsible for putting that look on your face again.

"I'd come up that day, ready to beg, crawl, plead, whatever it took. When I saw you kissing him, something snapped. I started thinking about the men you'd been with these past three years. The men who'd have you again when I couldn't."

"I've never been with any man but you," Autumn interrupted quietly.

Lucas's expression changed from barely suppressed fury to confusion before he studied her face with his familiar intensity. "Why?"

"Because every time I started to, I remembered he wasn't you."

As if in pain, Lucas shut his eyes, then turned from her. "Cat, I've never done anything in my life to deserve you."

"No, you probably haven't." She rose from the bed to stand behind him. "Lucas, if you want me, tell me so, and tell me why. Ask me, Lucas. I want it spelled out."

"All right." He moved his shoulders as he turned back, but his eyes weren't casual. "Cat..." He reached up to touch her cheek, then thrust the hand in his pocket. "I want you, desperately, because life isn't even tolerable without you. I need you because you are, and always were, the best part of my life. I love you for reasons it would take hours to tell you. Take me back, please. Marry me."

She wanted to throw herself into his arms, but held back. *Don't make it too easy on him.* Julia's words played back in her head. No, Lucas had had too much come too easily to him. Autumn smiled at him, but didn't reach out.

"All right," she said simply.

"All right?" He frowned, uncertain. "All right what?"

"I'll marry you. That's what you want, isn't it?"

"Yes, damn it, but—"

"The least you could do is kiss me, Lucas. It's traditional."

Lightly, he rested his hands on her shoulders. "Cat, I want you to be sure, because I'll never be able to let go. If it's gratitude, I'm desperate enough to take it. But I want you to think about what you're doing."

She tilted her head. "You did know I thought it was you with Helen on that film?"

"Cat, for God's sake—"

"I went into the woods," she continued mildly. "I was just about to expose that film when Steve found me. Lucas." She inched closer. "Do you know how I feel about the sanctity of film?"

His breath came out in a small huff of relief as he lifted a hand to either side of her face. He grinned. "Yes. Yes, I do. Something about the eleventh commandment."

"Thou shalt not expose unprocessed film. Now,"—she slid her arms up his back—"are you going to kiss me, or do I have to make you?"

*   *   *   *   *

YOU'VE ASKED FOR IT,
YOU'VE GOT IT! MAN OF
THE MONTH: 1992

ONLY FROM
SILHOUETTE® *Desire*™

You just couldn't get enough of them, those sexy men from Silhouette Desire—twelve sinfully sexy, delightfully devilish heroes. Some will make you sweat, some will make you sigh . . . but every long, lean one of them will have you swooning. So here they are, men we couldn't resist bringing to you for one more year. . . .

A KNIGHT IN TARNISHED ARMOR
by Ann Major in January

THE BLACK SHEEP
by Laura Leone in February

THE CASE OF THE MESMERIZING BOSS
by Diana Palmer in March

DREAM MENDER
by Sherryl Woods in April

WHERE THERE IS LOVE
by Annette Broadrick in May

BEST MAN FOR THE JOB
by Dixie Browning in June

Don't let these men get away! *Man of the Month*, only in Silhouette Desire.

From the popular author of the bestselling title
DUNCAN'S BRIDE (Intimate Moments #349)
comes the

LINDA HOWARD

COLLECTION

Two exquisite collector's editions that contain four of
Linda Howard's early passionate love stories. To add
these special volumes to your own library, be sure
to look for:

VOLUME ONE: *Midnight Rainbow*
Diamond Bay
(Available in March)

VOLUME TWO: *Heartbreaker*
White Lies
(Available in April)

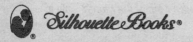 *Silhouette Books*®

SLH92

You, too, can write in the
LANGUAGE OF LOVE with Silhouette's

FREE
ELEGANT STATIONERY

An elegant box of stationery—perfect for yourself or to give as a gift! Each sheet is beautifully imprinted with specially commissioned artwork from the Nora Roberts Language of Love Collection. Every box includes 24 sheets, six each of four different designs, all in full color, plus 24 matching envelopes.

This stationery will not be sold in retail stores. See proof-of-purchase on next page for details. (Retail value of stationery: $12.95)

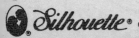

LOLSTA

NORA ROBERTS
LANGUAGE OF LOVE

FREE Floral Stationery

Just mail us four proofs-of-purchase from any of NORA ROBERTS Language of Love titles 1 to 12, plus $2.75 for postage and handling (check or money order—please do not send cash) payable to Silhouette Reader Service to:

In the U.S.

Language of Love Stationery
Silhouette Books
3010 Walden Avenue
P.O. Box 1396
Buffalo, NY 14269-1396

In Canada

Language of Love Stationery
Silhouette Books
P.O. Box 609
Fort Erie, Ontario
L2A 5X3

(offer expires September 31, 1992)

Please allow six weeks for delivery.

ORDER FORM

Name_____

Address_____ Apt._____

City_____ State/Prov._____

Daytime Phone #_____ Zip/Postal Code_____

Silhouette ®

✂ LANGUAGE OF LOVE
PROOF-OF-PURCHASE